WHERE THERE'S A WITCH, THERE'S A WAY

AN EIRA SNOW COZY MYSTERY (BOOK ONE)

Victoria DeLuis

For J.

With special thanks to my family and Aimee.

Published in 2020 by
Deryn Publishing
United Kingdom

First Edition

© 2020 Victoria DeLuis
www.victoriadeluis.com

All characters, places and events are fictional. Any resemblance to
real persons, places or events is purely coincidental.

The moral rights of the author have been asserted.

All rights reserved. No part of this publication may be reproduced, copied, stored
or distributed in any form, without prior written permission of the publisher.

CONTENTS

Chapter One	1
Chapter Two	9
Chapter Three	18
Chapter Four	40
Chapter Five	55
Chapter Six	72
Chapter Seven	76
Chapter Eight	89
Chapter Nine	102
Chapter Ten	115
Chapter Eleven	132
Chapter Twelve	138
Chapter Thirteen	149
Chapter Fourteen	158
Chapter Fifteen	166
Chapter Sixteen	179
Chapter Seventeen	183
Chapter Eighteen	192
Chapter Nineteen	199
Chapter One	207

CHAPTER ONE

As a witch, I'm used to the strange and unusual. It comes with the territory. Still, it's not every day you stumble across a dead body. But there she was, as plain as day and as dead as a person could be. There was no point checking for a pulse. The angle of the poor lady's neck told me there was no hope.

I pulled my phone from my bag, called the police, and waited for them to arrive. While I did, I couldn't help but notice the woman was around the same age as me. Forty-one was far too young to die. Other than in age, we didn't look that much the same at all. We were both tall and slim, but it was hard to judge her height, given the circumstances. She had bobbed hair, which was perfectly styled, her lips ruby red, whereas I tended to opt for minimal make-up and had long curly hair that ranged around my head with a mind of its own. Her dress was shorter than I'd ever dare to wear. Not that you'd find me in a dress at all these days.

Conscious of my recent divorce, my gaze drifted to her hand, searching for a wedding band. Instead, I noted that she'd had her manicured fingernails painted to match her lips and that they clenched tight to a piece of paper.

I shifted position and tilted my head to see what was written on it. My heart almost burst when I realised it was a poster, begging for information in relation to a lost cat by the name of Abby. A white floofball with a black tail and a few black patches on her fur. I grabbed a pen from my bag and used the end to push the paper straighter and almost fell on top of the poor woman when I gasped at the size of the reward offered.

Deciding it was best for my prying to come to an end, I backed towards the front door and away from the body. The sun was slowly setting and burnished the sky in a rich blend of orange and crimson, casting the dark hallway in a macabre light.

"Was Abby your cat or one you found?" I pondered out loud and shivered when a blast of air as cold as the depths of winter hit me.

A well of dread built inside, and the hairs on the back of my neck stood to attention.

"Abby's my little angel," a woman's voice said.

I gulped in a breath and tried to calm my racing heart whilst turning to look. The dead woman's spirit, dressed in the same black mini-dress and impossibly high heels as her body, stared down at me from the top of the stairs.

All the moisture left my throat, and I could barely form a coherent thought, let alone speak.

The ghost took each step towards me with agonising slowness, her phantom footsteps making no noise on the redwood stairs. Fear glued my own feet in place, and all I could do was stand and gape.

This wasn't my first encounter with a ghost. There was a time or two as a child when I'd tried to convince my father I'd seen one. Both times, the effort earned me a smacked bottom and a two-week grounding. That was all the lesson I needed. If you ignore something long enough, it's almost like it disappears. Just ask my ex-husband, Chris. To him, I was practically invisible, as a woman anyway. But ignoring the ghost that edged closer and closer proved impossible with the icy touch of her presence and the deathly stare of eyes that never blinked.

"I-is she missing?" I finally managed, my voice barely above a whisper. I sounded like an idiot. Of course, the cat was missing. I'd learnt that from the flyer not five minutes ago.

Before she had the chance to answer, two sets of blue flashing lights appeared outside, and in the blink of an eye, she vanished.

I took a deep breath, tried to shake the unease crawling up my spine, and stepped outside into the ever-darkening sky to greet the police. Within moments, I found myself in a flurry of activity. A plain-clothed officer turned on the outside light and started grilling me beneath its glare. She stood a couple of inches taller than me in a fitted navy suit. She had a warm and sunny touch to her face like a citrine gemstone, although that might have been the light. Her blonde hair was tied back in a simple low pony. The colour looked natural, but as I placed her around five years older than me, I surmised it couldn't be. I'd been dyeing the grey from my hair for a good four years and had no doubt she did too. Despite her questions and business-like manner, her blue eyes shone with caring.

"No. I don't know who the deceased is," I said in answer to her latest question, trying hard not to roll my eyes with her third time asking it.

"Then why are you at her house?"

Once again, I pointed to the neighbouring house and explained how I'd noticed the open door whilst delivering a package to its owner.

I'd only recently moved to the quaint village of Caerleon

in South Wales and opened Crystal Magic, a spiritual shop located down the road from the Roman Fortress and Baths, and I was keen for the locals to sample my concoctions and reap their benefits. Although I had a good income from selling my remedies online and didn't need to rely on foot traffic for my trade, I couldn't think of a better way to become a staple of the community and meet new people than running a physical store.

The store and accompanying cottage were something of an impulse purchase following my divorce. I'd been browsing online when I'd stumbled upon them. You might say, perusing property sites, looking at the fancy houses, and seeing how all the rich people lived was a hobby of mine. I called it 'lottery-shopping'. My ex called it a waste of time. The business was in my price range, and the idea of finding a place to call home in the village of my birth appealed in more ways than one.

The deceased's neighbour was Samantha Jenkins. My one and only customer to date. She was a small grey-haired woman with glasses, carnelian-red kissed cheeks, and a homely look about her. Her eyes were puffy and swollen when she'd popped into my store just before closing and purchased a fusion of peppermint and eucalyptus oil to help with allergies and a smoke-cleansing kit.

"I know your remedies are for humans, but do you think you could whip something up to calm my neighbour's cat? The poor thing is terribly anxious," she'd said as she was leaving. "I'll be out, but if you could pop it over later and leave it on the doorstep under the porch, I'll come around tomorrow to pay for it."

"That won't be a problem," I'd replied.

Yeah, no problem at all. Of course, I didn't have to investigate when I saw the open door. That was all on me.

I'd soon found Mrs Jenkins' modern detached house with the green garage door from the directions she gave me. Baskets filled with daffodils hung on either side of the front door from the porch that covered it. As instructed, I left the oil on the doorstep and turned to go home, wondering which of her neighbours had the stressed-out cat.

As I left her drive, I looked at the other houses in the area. All were of a similar design: detached houses with built-in garages and dormer style windows in the upstairs. There were only around twelve of them, and it was clear they'd all been built at the same time as part of a development. It was then that I noticed the door on the house to the right of Mrs Jenkins' was ajar.

I stopped short. The house was practically screaming out to me with alarm bells sounding in my head. I stood and stared at it for a few minutes, looking for any sign of movement. The air felt strange, as though it compressed around the house in a cloud of anguish. I shivered and clutched my handbag tighter.

There was nothing good about the open door, of that, I was certain. I pushed my shoulders back and steeled myself before entering the garden and edging towards the house, calling out, "Hello," in the process. Dread built like a kick to the gut with the unwavering certainty of what I'd find inside. The sensor light flared to life, almost blinding me, but I'd continued.

I stood under the glare of that same light now and explained everything to the detective. Well... not everything. I fully intended to keep the bit about the ghostly apparition to myself.

She eyed me warily as though she sensed I was holding something back. "I'm going to need your name and address," she said after a moment. "And I'd like you to give a statement to one of my officers."

"Of course. I'm Eira Snow." I perked up, thinking I may get home sometime tonight after all. "Might I ask your name?" I asked, resigned to the idea that this wouldn't be the end of my discussions with the police.

"Detective Inspector Kate McIntyre," she answered before handing me a business card and waving another officer over to take my details. She left to see inside the house without so much as a backward glance.

I tossed her card in my bag and shivered as the first drop of rain hit me square on the nose. Great! My shoulders slumped, and I glanced up the road. A stiff drink was calling. As I wistfully wished to already be home in front of the TV with a glass of gin in my hand and my cat, Niles curled on my lap, I noticed a flash of white jump on the garden wall and dart with lightning speed inside a bush.

CHAPTER TWO

"Abby!" I exclaimed, much to the surprise of the officer who had arrived to take my details. "The missing cat." I elaborated by waving my hand like a maniac at the bush.

"Abby," Tanya echoed, appearing beside me.

I jumped in surprise, earning me a quizzical look from the officer. He could look at me funny all he wanted. I wasn't the one practically standing on top of a ghost. I wondered if he felt the strange tingling sensation in the air at Tanya's presence, but shrugged the thought away and focused on walking slowly to the bush and crouching low.

"Come here, Abby," I said, seeing the pink of her nose and a touch of white through the dense leaves as she bunched at the very back against the wall. "There's a good girl. I won't hurt you."

Tanya knelt beside me. Abby must have seen her too, as she relaxed and inched forward. Tanya reached out to grab the cat. The sobbing gasp that came from her throat when her hands went straight through the bundle of floof almost broke my heart. To save her more heartache, I gathered the tiny bundle in my arms and lifted her from the ground.

She was a bag of bones beneath the floof. "Oh, baby, you must be starving. How long have you been missing?" I asked, more of Tanya than the cat, although as none of the police could see the ghost and I had no intention of telling them she was there, it seemed otherwise.

"Four days. I've been so worried." Tanya choked back a sob. "What will happen to my sweet angel now that I'm… well, you know, dead?"

Relief washed through me. *Thank goodness for small mercies!* I had so not been looking forward to living *The Sixth Sense* and having to convince Tanya she was dead, and that 'I see dead people'.

I glanced at her, staring down at her angel, and sighed. The fact that she cared so much for her cat made me think we might have been friends had she lived.

"Um, excuse me," I said to the officer. "I think this cat

belongs here. Is there anyone that can take care of her?"

Tanya stretched her hand towards Abby but froze an inch or two before reaching her. "There's no one who'd have her," she said.

Before the officer had a chance to respond, the Detective Inspector emerged from the house. She must have heard my question as she said, "Records indicate the deceased as the sole occupant. We will inform her next of kin of the accident—"

A string of expletives from Tanya drowned out anything else she might have said. "Accident, what *bleeping* accident?" she added before placing both hands on her hips and calling the DI every name under the sun. Okay, she didn't use the word bleeping. My ex liked to swear at me a lot, and over the years, I'd learnt to temper the blow by censoring his words in my head.

I cleared my throat and raised an eyebrow at her, hoping she would get my message and stay quiet so I could think for a second. When she finally settled down, I took a deep breath, apologised for my questions, and asked Kate if she really believed the death to be an accident.

She looked at me curiously for a while. "It certainly looks that way," she said after a moment. "Her heel is broken."

Tanya's ghost stumbled to the side, squealing as she fell through the officer next to her.

Yuck! I shuddered, picturing ectoplasm as a giant blob of

gloop that had just coated the officer inside and out in invisible slime. I'd need a shower as well as a glass of gin to stop my skin from crawling.

Tanya cussed again and looked at her feet with a scowl on her face. She removed the shoe from her left foot and studied the heel. Moments before, it had been complete. Now, it hung from the sole by a thread. She tutted and took off her second shoe and flung both viciously to the ground. I winced at the imagined sound of them shattering, but as they weren't corporeal, the instant they left Tanya's hands, they vanished.

"It looks like this caused her to fall down the stairs," Kate continued, not having witnessed Tanya's little huff.

"I may have *bleeping* fallen down the *bleeping* stairs," Tanya placed her hands on her hips and glared at the DI. "But I was *bleeping* pushed. You'd better tell her that."

Yay! I'd better tell her that! My head hurt, and the cat was getting bored in my arms. I shifted Abby a little so that she sat over my shoulder but made sure to keep a tight hold of her so she wouldn't run away.

"I mean, an accident," I said, not sure how to phrase anything so as not to cause offence or raise suspicion. I sucked in a deep breath before continuing, "The door was open, and what about the missing cat flyer in her hand? Isn't that a little odd?"

DI Kate McIntyre walked up to me with her head cocked

slightly to the side, the way a dog does when it's questioning your actions. "Is there something you'd like to confess?" she asked, stopping a couple of inches from my face and eyeballing me.

"No, of course not," I blustered. "I was just thinking how strange it was that the door was open, and she had a flyer for her missing cat in her hand." I felt silly repeating myself, but I couldn't think of any other way to get my point across. "Don't you?" I added, more of a pleading that she should agree than an actual question.

"The cat you're holding. She doesn't look like she's missing to me."

I petted Abby on the head and held her tighter, if such a thing were possible. "She's not missing *now*, but from the flyer, it's clear she was."

"Maybe the deceased was rushing to create flyers for her missing cat and that's why her heel broke, and she fell down the stairs," interjected the officer, who had still to take my details.

Kate silenced him with a look. He cleared his throat, took out a little pad and pen, and pretended to focus on something else.

My mind went into overdrive, and words tumbled from my mouth. "If she was making the flyers, wouldn't there be more than one?" I said. "Shouldn't you check if someone could have wanted her dead? Like a boyfriend or something. Someone who could have keys. The lock wasn't broken and there was no key in it. Although maybe… maybe someone came to collect the reward and she didn't have it, so they kill—"

Kate raised her hand to silence me. "This is not an Agatha Christie novel and you are not Miss Marple. Unless you have something to tell me, Officer Johnson will take your details and you are free to leave."

Tanya huffed out a non-existent breath and shook her head. "Oh, what do I *bleeping* care, anyway?" she said and scowled at the detective. "It's not as if it will make a difference to me. The only important thing now is to make sure Abby's taken care of."

"What will happen to the cat?" I asked.

Kate nodded to Officer Johnson, who held out his hand to take her from me. I stepped back. She gave a deep, resolved sigh. "The cat will be taken to the council cattery and kept until someone claims her."

"Noooo," Tanya wailed. "She hates those places. No one will ever come. You absolutely cannot let them take her."

I petted the soft floofball on the head and rubbed her fur with my chin, eliciting a soft purr. "Would it be possible for me to take her home? You could fetch her from there if anyone comes forward to claim her. I'll keep her safe. She's been through enough already. I'd hate to think of her going through any more needless stress. I have a cat of my own and will take great care of her."

"Of course you do," Kate muttered under her breath.

I ignored the meaningless slight and gave her a pleading look. In the end, the caring nature I believed buried beneath her gruff exterior won through, and she agreed to my request.

I smiled and thanked her before giving all my details to Officer Johnson at breakneck speed. After safely securing Abby in my oversized bag, I started the short walk home.

"I can't thank you enough." Tanya's ghostly apparition walked by my side. Without her heels, she appeared a little shorter than my five-foot-seven. "I can already tell how much Abby likes you. She can't stand most *bleeping* people."

I smiled and nodded, but waited until we were far enough away from the house to say anything for fear of looking like a crazy person. I'd done enough of that this evening already. Even then, before speaking, I pulled my phone from my bag, gave the cat a quick pet in the process, and pretended to be on a call.

"Were you really pushed?" I asked.

"What…? Yes. Definitely. There's no doubting I was pushed. But, as I said, the only thing that matters is Abby, and you've got her. You will make sure she's safe and happy?"

"Of course, I will." From the corner of my eye, I noted that Tanya seemed to be fading. I had to squint to see her properly. It was like focusing on one of the magic eye pictures that were popular back in the 90s. When she'd disappeared earlier, she had vanished in a poof of nothing, but now her body was becoming more and more translucent. I didn't know exactly what that meant, but there was also a strange warming of the air that seemed out of place for the chill April night, and I wondered if Tanya had concluded her unfinished business and was moving on.

To answer my question, she stopped dead (pardon the pun) in her tracks and reached her hand out in front of her. "Julie," she said as tears formed in her eyes. "It's been so long. Can you ever forgive me?"

A young woman, no more than eighteen, appeared before us. Her long black hair flowed in some unfelt breeze. "There's nothing to forgive," she said and smiled. "I've been waiting for you."

"I love you so much." Tears fell freely down Tanya's face. "I've missed you every single day."

"I know. But you don't have to be lonely anymore."

"But I did nothing. I knew, and I did nothing."

Julie reached her hand out. "It doesn't matter. We can be together forever. No one can stop us."

I wiped a tear from my own eye and watched as a feeling of poignancy washed through me. Tanya clasped onto Julie's hand, and they both disappeared.

I stood for a moment wondering who would come to me when I died, but shook the thought away when a few more raindrops splattered on my face. Unlike Tanya, I would have far too much unfinished business to move on so quickly. It would likely be decades after my point of death before I could cross over into the next realm of existence. I really needed to sort my life out to prevent that from happening.

I delved my hand inside my bag and stroked Abby while speed-walking the rest of the way home, hoping to avoid the worst of the rain. The first bit of unfinished business I had to deal with was Tanya's killer. She might not care one bit if they were caught or not, but I certainly did. The idea of a murderer running free around my new village home wasn't one that settled well inside my stomach.

I just wished I had the faintest idea of how to go about finding them. As Detective Inspector Kate McIntyre had kindly informed me, I was no Miss Marple. But as my mother used to say, where there's a witch, there's a way. I could only hope that proved true in this instance.

CHAPTER THREE

I felt like hell when I dragged myself from bed the next morning. My head pounded, every part of my body ached, and all I wanted to do was go back to bed and sleep the day away.

To say Niles hadn't taken kindly to Abby's presence would be an understatement. Not that I could blame him. We were bonded on my first birthday and he hadn't left my side since. Nor would he. Ever. As my familiar, his life was tied to mine, and he would live however long I did. You might say that we belonged to each other, but as he will forever at heart be a cat, it's more the case that I belong to him. And Niles does not like to share.

They screeched, yowled, and hissed. My eardrums seemed

fit to burst. In the end, I settled poor Abby alone in the bedroom of the flat above the shop for the night, just so I could grab a couple of hours sleep.

I sleepwalked down the stairs and grumbled as I popped the kettle on before taking a seat at the breakfast bar. My head dropped to the counter and my eyes drifted closed. Niles butted my head with his and turned to whip me with his tail. He generated a loud purr and repeated the act a few more times. I whimpered and lifted my head from the table.

"It's your fault I'm this tired," I said while he nuzzled my face, making me spit black hairs from my lips. I rubbed him behind the ear and under the chin. "Okay," I huffed. "I'm awake. I'll feed you."

I stretched my back, set Niles out a bowl of food, and clicked the kettle to boil again. After breakfast, consisting of a banana muffin and magically infused ginseng tea for energy, I showered, dressed, and applied enough make-up to pass as a human being. No mean feat under the circumstances. Grabbing a second bowl of cat food from the kitchen, I headed to the store and climbed the stairs to the flat above in search of Abby. But as soon as I opened the bedroom door, she darted down the stairs and the screeching and yowling began again.

I huffed out a deep breath and trudged back down to find that Niles had followed me from the main house.

The two cats faced each other in a standoff. Abby's black tail was fluffed to three times its normal size, her back was arched, and her ears flattened tight on her head. She stood between the comfortable sofa and one of the two overstuffed armchairs that sat around the coffee table in the centre of the room. Not normal items to find in a shop, but I'd wanted to make the store as homely and inviting as possible. Niles had decided to act all innocent and perched his bottom on the arm of the sofa whilst giving Abby an appraising look. I glanced from Niles to Abby and back again. In the blink of an eye, Niles changed. He'd grown, and no longer resembled a healthy domesticated cat, instead he'd taken on the appearance and size of a panther. He extended his claws.

"Don't even think about it," I said and lifted my finger in warning.

Without hesitating, I used my magic to gather Abby from the floor and swooshed her out of the store and back up the stairs to the flat. Her breakfast bowl floated behind her. I deposited them both on the ground and closed the door to keep her locked in before turning my attention to Niles.

"Abby is a guest in our house," I said, giving him my best you'd-better-listen glare. "She's had a hard time of late. You will be nice. Understand?"

Niles fixed me with his emerald green eyes, returned to his

normal form, and turned to look at the door of the shop.

My heart thundered, and a rock sank into the pit of my stomach. Outside the door and looking through the glass window was a young woman with warm brown skin tinged with a little grey like smoky quartz and the enviable cheekbones of Thandie Newton. A shocked yet strangely elated look brightened her face. It was then that I realised she must have witnessed my small magic feat as well as Niles' shifting ability.

I closed my eyes and willed her to be gone. But instead of disappearing, the woman started banging on the door and calling my name.

"Eira, that is you, isn't it?" she said in a thick Bristolian accent, which seemed to add a 'wl' to the end of my name. "It's me. Fleur Evans."

"Fleur?" *Fleur!* She might just be the worst person to have witnessed my oversight.

Although we'd never met in person, Fleur and I had engaged in numerous conversations online. Without a profile picture to go on, I'd assumed her to be older, late twenties maybe, rather than the eighteen or nineteen she must be. Fleur had purchased a moonstone pendulum spelled to enhance intuition and help someone find success and good fortune. Unfortunately, I hadn't counted on her focusing her intuition on my abilities. She became convinced I was a 'real' witch, and it took quite a bit of persuasion on my part to make her think otherwise. Something that had flown straight out the window with my moment's lapse in judgement.

I opened my eyes and glanced around the room, looking for something that might help. Shelving lined the walls adorned with incense and herbs, which stood side by side with healing crystals and magical potions bonded to essential oils. The shop was pristine and ordered just how I liked it. As always, a vase of beautiful fresh-cut flowers stood on the coffee table next to a bowl of sherbet lemons that visitors were more than welcome to delve into and retrieve a sweet or two. A mix of delicious scents hung in the air like fruit and flowers, or the fresh ozone of a rainstorm on a summer's day. There had to be something...

Fleur knocked on the door again.

"I blame you for this," I muttered to Niles as I walked over to open it.

Fleur pushed past me and rushed towards my familiar. She circled around and stared at him as though he was the eighth wonder of the world. I debated the possibility of mixing a spell to make her forget. Rosemary and lemon balm oil were both good for memory. It was possible I could reverse their effects and... I shook the idea from my head. Doing such a thing would be... well, it would be very rude, and not like me at all. I'd be better off trying to talk my way out of things.

"What did you just do to that cat?" Fleur almost squealed, her voice bubbling over with excitement.

I sighed, left the 'closed' sign on display, and locked back up. "What cat?" I asked, knowing how stupid the words were the second they left my mouth. If I was going to convince Fleur that she hadn't seen anything, I'd have to do better than that.

Fleur bounced from foot to foot. "What cat?" she echoed and pointed at him. "This cat. What other cat is there?"

"Oh, *this* cat." To be honest, despite my ginseng tea, my mind wasn't working at full speed this morning. My magic never worked as well for me as it did for other people. If it did, I wouldn't have to 'lottery shop' for a big fancy house, I'd just shop. Still, it suddenly dawned on me that I might not be in as much trouble here as I'd thought. "I can, hand on heart swear that I just did nothing to this cat," I said and roved my eyes over Fleur. She wore a white ribbed top with denim shorts, black tights, and ankle boots. And dangling around her neck resided the pendulum I'd sold her. With any luck, her enhanced intuition would show her the truth in my words. "What are you doing here?" I asked to move the conversation along to what I hoped would be a safer topic.

Fleur ran her hand over her obsidian-black pixie cut. "I passed the other day. When I saw the Crystal Magic sign, I wondered if I might find you here."

"Well, I guess you have your answer. Sherbet lemon?" I offered, pointing to the bowl on the table and shooing Niles off the sofa. He left, edging through the beaded curtains to the small kitchen area behind the till and out the back door to the cottage, swishing his tail in displeasure. We'd be having words about his attitude later — I sighed — not that it would do any good.

Fleur grabbed a sweetie and sat down on the seat Niles vacated. "I need you to take me on as an apprentice witch," she said, as though there was no room for disagreement. "You can teach me how to change a cat into a leopard or vice versa."

"Fleur, we've been through this." I took the seat opposite her and tried not to roll my eyes. "I have never changed a cat into a leopard or into anything else, for that matter. I'm no more of a witch than you are."

She smiled. A far too sly smile that spoke volumes and made my jaw clench. She pointed her finger at the bowl of sherbet lemons. Her face strained and sweat broke out on her brow.

I gasped, sensing the magic in the air. It didn't flow in its natural state. More like thick tar than free-flowing energy, or the jittery stop start of an engine when the exhaust backfires, but it was there.

After a few seconds, one of the sweets shook. It trembled amongst the other immobile sweets and rose into the air just a couple of inches before it fell back into the bowl. Fleur panted as though she'd just run a marathon and leaned forward with her hands on her knees, trying to catch her breath.

I sat dumbfounded, my mouth gaping open. "H-how?" I said after a moment.

Fleur shrugged. "When I realised you were a real witch, I did some research online. It seemed to me that a lot of magic relies on fixing the thing you want in your mind and believing it will happen." She clutched the pendulum around her neck. "The same way you said this worked."

"I see," I said and nodded. That was the way things worked, for the most part, but I'd never heard of a witch coming into her powers so late. As a rule, witches are born to other witches. It's much easier to do magic when you've been trained from birth to know it's possible. Any shred of self-doubt and a spell simply will not work. "Wow, you have an impressive belief in your own abilities," I muttered to myself more than to Fleur.

"Not in my abilities," she said, and looked sheepishly at her feet. "In yours. I just knew you were a witch. As I knew magic could be done, I decided there was no reason I couldn't do it too."

"Let me get this straight. As soon as you knew it was possible to manipulate the world, you just had to free your mind and accept that you too had the ability to do it? Kind of like Neo in *The Matrix*."

"Who?"

"Neo. You know, Keanu Reeves. *The Matrix.*"

"The guy from *John Wick*?"

I flopped my head in my hands and rubbed at my temple. "Never mind. It was a poor example, anyway." I shuddered, suddenly feeling incredibly old. "What else can you do?" I asked.

"Nothing. That's why I need you to teach me."

I studied Fleur. She really was very pretty. At almost twenty, she was late to the game, but still young. The fact that she'd been able to levitate the sherbet lemon with no training whatsoever was beyond impressive. Who knew what she'd be capable of if I did teach her? For that matter, who knew what she'd be capable of if I didn't? I just... I'd never thought about taking on an apprentice. I'd dreamed of having a daughter and passing on my knowledge, but the time limit on achieving that feat was fast closing in.

I looked at Fleur. Her deep brown eyes, lined with thick black liner and accented with a golden eyeshadow, almost popped out of her head. Her expectant face brimmed with hope and determination.

"Fine," I said after a moment, smiling. "I'll teach you everything I know."

Fleur jumped out of her seat and pulled me from mine, dragging me into a great bear hug and jumping up and down with me in her arms. "I knew you were a witch," she almost squealed and pulled away, smiling. "Where do I start?"

"You start by learning the properties of essential oils and crystals," I said. "You can—"

A knock on the door silenced me. I cursed and vowed to get some sort of shutter system in place to stop people from seeing in. Although, maybe drawing the lilac curtains that matched the rug and draped the two large windows would be a good place to start. Not that we'd been caught at magic. This time. But had the knock come a few minutes sooner, my second unexpected visitor would have seen Fleur levitate the sherbet lemon.

The scowl on my face soon shifted when I turned to see an incredibly handsome man waving at me through the window.

Butterflies flip-flopped in the pit of my stomach and fluttered all the way into my chest. Did I mention he was incredibly handsome? It took every ounce of restraint I had to not stand with my mouth agape, drooling. His face was strong and defined, with a jawline to rival Henry Cavill's, and his dark brown hair had the type of lustrous, tousled curls on top that made me itch to thread my fingers through them.

"Ooh, who's the Adonis?" Fleur asked, nudging me with her elbow.

I blushed and moved to open the door. And then stood, blocking the way without saying a word, when the newcomer looked at me intently. I realised I was staring into his perfect blue, sparkling eyes and shifted my gaze. It rested on his broad chest and the navy-blue jumper stretched tightly across it. I swallowed. Suddenly, I was conscious of my appearance, and my simple white button-down top and jeans, which did nothing to accentuate my figure. Although, on occasion, I liked to think my bottom looked quite good in jeans. And my hair... oh my hair, goodness knew what my hair was doing. I rushed my hand up to smooth it down and brush the loose, wavy curls over my shoulder. Then froze, worried that touching my hair might be construed as flirting.

Was it flirting? Was *I* flirting?

I was only just getting used to the idea of being single. I couldn't be flirting. The heat in my cheeks intensified and my chest tightened. I looked at my feet, wondering how on earth they had managed to stay rooted to the spot when every instinct told me to flee.

Fleur came up behind me and cleared her throat. "Can we help?" she asked, rescuing me from myself.

"I'm Aaron Jenkins. My mother asked me to pop in and pay for the oil you delivered last night."

"Aaron Jenkins." I took a step back. "Of course, Samantha Jenkins' son. How is your mother today? Have her allergies cleared up?"

"She's fine." Aaron smiled and held out his hand in greeting.

"You must be Eira Snow," he said in a voice that could melt butter.

I tentatively shook his hand and tried to ignore the tingles that flushed up my arm.

Fleur bobbed on her tiptoes and waved. "I'm Fleur," she said. "Eira's apprentice."

"It's a pleasure to meet you, Fleur." Aaron shook her hand and walked into the shop. My eyes drifted down his body and I sighed. His was definitely a bottom that looked good in jeans.

Fleur fanned her face and mouthed, '*Wow.*'

Wow, indeed. I smirked and blushed some more whilst trying to get my racing heart under control. For goodness' sake, anyone would think I was a teenager with the way I was acting and not a forty-one-year-old woman.

Aaron turned and focused all his attention on me. "I need to pay for the oil you left at Mum's. She didn't feel like leaving the house this morning and shooed me away from her house when I called over." He leaned forward and whispered in my ear. "She also mentioned you were exceptionally beautiful. But I must confess, I didn't quite believe her until I walked through the door." I swallowed. "Plus," he added, pulling back, "she was a little concerned about you after what happened last night and wanted me to make sure you were okay."

"What happened last night?" Fleur asked, moving up behind

me.

"I found a murder victim."

"Murder?" Fleur and Aaron both said at the same time, although Fleur with much more enthusiasm.

Aaron scrunched his face in confusion. "Mum said it was an accident. Tanya fell down the stairs."

I huffed out a breath. With everything that had happened between the cats and then Fleur appearing, I hadn't thought about what to do in relation to Tanya's murder. There was no way I could leave it alone, but I still didn't have the faintest idea where to start. I shook my head. "It was murder. I know it."

"But the police—"

"If Eira said it was murder, then it was murder," Fleur said, standing tall and challenging Aaron to disagree with her.

I turned to face her and smiled. It was nice of someone to have my back for a change. Maybe I'd get used to having an apprentice sooner than anticipated. "Thank you," I said.

Aaron rested his hand on my shoulder, and I savoured his sweet, woody aroma that seemed somehow familiar. "I'm a firm believer in following my gut, and if yours tells you Tanya was murdered, then I believe you." He stepped to the side and looked between me and Fleur as though thinking. "Why don't we pop to the café along the road for some breakfast and a cup of coffee? We can talk about it there. Fleur can take care of the store. Can't you Fleur?"

"I couldn't possibly." I said.

"I'll be fine," Fleur said and winked at me. "What else are apprentices for?"

My stomach rolled. I didn't even know Aaron Jenkins and hadn't been for coffee with a man besides my husband in more than twenty years. And I could count on one hand the times I'd done it with him. I mean, Aaron wasn't asking me on a date. I'd been out of the game for a long time, but even I knew that. It was just... he was *so* mind-bogglingly gorgeous, and the thought of dating just popped into my mind. On top of that, I was pretty certain Aaron had called me beautiful. Something else that hadn't happened in twenty years.

"I couldn't possibly," I said again.

"Of course you can." Fleur raised her eyebrows, making her eyes look like they might pop out of her head. She nodded towards the door and mouthed, 'go'.

"I insist," Aaron added, unaware of Fleur's actions. "It'll do you good to talk things through and sort your thoughts. Nothing fuels the mind better than a good breakfast."

Despite having eaten a banana muffin, I had to admit, I was still a little hungry, and a more substantial breakfast wouldn't go amiss. Plus, I rationalised, Aaron might know something about Tanya that could give me a place to start in finding her killer.

I thanked Fleur and told her to go online while she was watching the store and read up on the products I stocked in my online shop and all their properties.

She nodded, and I grabbed my bag and purse and followed Aaron along the road to the local café, doing my best not to fidget and look nervous. The café was only a few doors down, through large blue gates and on a cobbled alleyway. We didn't have time to chat as we walked, but I did have the chance to thank Aaron for checking in on me.

"It's my pleasure," he said. "And I still have to pay for the oil you dropped off at Mum's last night."

I smiled. "How about you pay for breakfast and we call it quits?"

Aaron pushed the door open for me, and we entered. Inside, the café was small but bright and airy, with a friendly atmosphere.

"As I fully intended on paying for breakfast already, I'll take you out for dinner tonight in lieu of payment."

The churning in my stomach increased as the waitress directed us to a table at the far end of the room and we took our seats. "Can I get you any drinks?" she asked, while handing us the breakfast menu.

Aaron looked at me expectantly. I ordered a peppermint tea while he opted for a double espresso. Neither of us moved for a heartbeat after she left until Aaron opened his menu.

"Eggs Benedict sounds good to me," he said.

I took a deep breath and perused my own menu, debating whether to have the Avocado and Smoked Salmon, which came with halloumi, as well as tomatoes and poached egg on toast, but as it sounded like a lot of food and I'd already had a muffin, I opted for Eggs Royale instead.

"What made you decide to move to Caerleon?" Aaron asked after our drinks arrived and we'd ordered.

"I was born here," I answered. "I moved away when I was nine after my mum died."

"Oh, I am sorry to hear that."

"Can't be helped." I took a sip of my peppermint tea and glanced around the café. Only a few other tables were occupied, and they were on the other side of the small room. "Anyway," I said, placing my cup back on the table, "I was searching for a fresh start after my divorce, found the shop for sale, and thought, why not? I'd always wanted to come back to my ancestral home, so to speak."

"How are you liking things so far? I hope finding Tanya's body hasn't tainted your view of the village."

"Not at all."

Our discussion stuck to pleasantries while we waited for our food to arrive. Aaron now lived in Newport, the neighbouring city. He and his parents had moved to the village almost twenty-five years ago. His dad died a few years after that. Aaron was an insurance claims adjuster for a firm in the city centre, but he'd booked the week off work to help his mum with a few things around the house. Something they'd had planned for a while.

"Although," he added, "She couldn't get me away from her house fast enough on Monday and hasn't needed me since. I'm guessing whatever she needed me to do isn't as pressing anymore."

We fell silent while we enjoyed our food. The homemade Hollandaise sauce that accompanied my poached eggs and smoked salmon was divine, and I wondered if the chef would be willing to part with the recipe.

"Did you know your mother's neighbour well?" I asked as soon as our plates were cleared away and another drink delivered.

The smile dropped from Aaron's face, making me sorry that I'd brought the subject up again. "I spoke to her occasionally when I visited Mum," he said. "I also have to confess. We went out on a few dates a couple of years back."

"You did?" My mind drifted to my brief interaction with Tanya. Her language was somewhat colourful, but she'd been lovely and doted on Abby. I resisted a sigh, but deflated a little inside. We still couldn't have been more different. If Aaron had a type, I certainly wasn't it.

Aaron took a large swig of coffee and leaned back in his chair. "It was just after my divorce. Her husband, Phill, passed away a few years earlier. He was a nice chap. A fair bit older than Tanya."

"Did they have any children?"

"Yes. A son. Benjamin. He's at University in Cardiff."

"He is?" My confusion must have shown on my face as Aaron asked me what was wrong. "Nothing. It's just, I have Tanya's cat —"

"Abby."

"Yes, Abby. The police wanted to put her into a cattery, but I thought it best she came home with me instead and they agreed. I was under the impression there would be no one to take care of her."

Aaron sat forward and clasped his hand on the table in front of him while I finished the last dregs of my second cup of tea. "I doubt Benjamin will take Abby in," he said. "He's not much of a cat person and always moaned about Tanya favouring the cat over him. There's Tanya's sister and her husband. They live in Ponthir, the next village along. If Mum didn't have a cat allergy, I would have said she would be happy to take her. She puts out a bowl of food every day for that cat to nibble on."

I nodded and wondered if Tanya's son or sister could be her

killer. Neither idea appealed.

Aaron finished his coffee and paid the bill. "Would you like to take a walk around the common?" he asked as we were leaving.

"I'd love to. Can I just pop in and see if Fleur's okay first?" I didn't know why I wasn't more worried about the situation with Fleur but given our past communication and our brief interaction that morning, I felt I could trust her. At least, I hoped I could. I'd like to say I was a good judge of character, but my ex had proved that to be untrue.

We exited through the blue gates back onto the main street, and Aaron stopped in his tracks. "Hold on," he said, pointing at the building opposite. Scaffolding surrounded its walls as well as a temporary plywood fence. I followed the trace of his finger and noted that amongst the posters advertising numerous events and businesses on the fence, there was a flyer, the spitting image of the one I'd seen in Tanya's hand the night before.

Aaron waited for a car to pass, then darted across the road and grabbed the flyer. A movement on the roof caught my eye, and I glanced up just in time to see a large part of the chimney fall towards where Aaron was standing.

Everything happened as if in slow motion. My chest tightened around my sluggish heartbeat. I shouted, "Look out!" The words echoed in my ears.

Aaron glanced upwards, but it was obvious he wouldn't move in time. I focused my magic and shifted the falling debris just enough to make it miss him. He stood shell-shocked as the bricks smashed on the floor beside him, sending a cloud of dust in the air. With the deafening impact, time returned to normal.

Not wanting to give Aaron space to think, I darted across the road, grabbed hold of his hand, and pulled him a few more steps to the side.

"Oh, my goodness," I said. "I really thought that was going to hit you."

"Me too." Aaron huffed and shook his head in disbelief. "You almost had a second dead body on your hands for a moment there."

He tried to make light of the situation, but the colour had drained from his face and instead of his normal flush of brown jasper, the gemstone he now resembled was more the greyish-white of the Spodumene.

"I have something in the store to help with shock," I said and glanced back at the smashed bricks a few steps away. "We'd better call the council and tell them about the hazard. It's a miracle no one's been hurt. They'll have to do something more than erect a little scaffolding. I know I haven't been here long, but I swear I've never seen a single person working on this building."

"What did you find?" I asked as I guided Aaron across the street, hoping that the flyer would give him something else to focus on. He handed it to me. "Tanya had the same thing in her hand when I found her last night," I said and stared at the image of Abby. "Do you think Tanya's sister would want to take her in?"

"The Cat? Trisha? I don't know." Aaron shook his head, and I heard the doubt in his voice.

"Maybe Benjamin will surprise you and want her."

"Maybe." Aaron glanced back at the derelict building before shaking his head again and sighing. "We could go and ask him. I wouldn't mind checking up and seeing if he's alright. I got the impression Tanya wasn't close to her sister, so he might need a hand with the funeral arrangements. It might be an idea to call in and see her sister at some point, too."

"That's very kind of you," I said.

Aaron turned to me and smiled. "Well, if we're going to investigate Tanya's murder, learning what we can from her family would be a good place to start."

"Do you really believe me when I say Tanya was murdered?" I asked. "Even though the police are looking at her death as an accident."

Aaron huffed out a breath. "If there was ever anyone I could see being murdered, it may seem strange to say, but that would be Tanya."

"Really? Why?"

"She liked to live life in the fast lane. Dated a lot of men, following her husband's death, and not always one at a time."

"Is that why you broke up?" I asked as we came to a stop outside the shop.

Aaron shook his head. "We just weren't on the same wavelength," he said before holding the door open for me to walk through.

CHAPTER FOUR

Fleur jumped up from behind the sofa and closed the laptop as soon as we entered. I was happy to see Abby curled up next to her but chose not to comment on the cat's appearance and instead asked her how her reading was going.

"All good," she said. "I've read through everything on the essential oils on your site and was just about to start on the crystals."

I smiled and suggested Aaron take a seat. He did, stating that he would call his mum and get Benjamin's address. I pulled Fleur behind the beaded curtains and into the back room.

"He's had a bit of a shock," I explained without going into

any details. "Which essential oil do you think would help?"

Fleur squinted her left eye for a second as though thinking and then beamed a great big smile at me. "Lavender," she said with confidence.

I smiled back. "Exactly."

"What happened?" she asked.

"I'll explain everything later when we're alone."

I peeked between the beaded curtain and around the arched doorway into the store. Aaron was talking on the phone. I couldn't hear the conversation on the other end, but from the look on Aaron's face, it was not going well.

"He's a good kid, Mum," he said while rubbing at his closed eyes. "His mother has just died. He might need a friend, someone to talk to."

I leaned against the wall and listened as he went on, explaining how much she meant to him and how devastated he'd be without her. It was clear that Aaron was close to his mother and everything I'd seen or heard from him made me believe him to be a kind and caring man. A far cry from my ex, who only ever thought about himself. I had no idea what was happening between us. I mean, he'd taken me for breakfast and basically said he'd be taking me for dinner tonight, too. But was he just being neighbourly or was this the way people started dating these days? I honestly had no idea, and there was no way

I could ask. I sighed and rubbed at my own eyes. Things were so much easier when I was young. I'd just go for a night out on the town with friends and wind up kissing someone. After that, if they called, it was assumed we were dating. Now, with dating apps and goodness knows what, I didn't have a clue how things were meant to work.

Fleur flicked the kettle on and offered to make us all a nice cup of tea. Thanking her, I fetched the lavender oil I'd already spelled to help with shock and pain relief from the shelf.

I smiled at Aaron, who was busy writing something down on the back of the receipt he'd gotten after paying for breakfast, grabbed the oil, and sat in the chair next to his.

"This, along with a nice cup of tea, will have you feeling yourself in no time," I said, popping the bottle top and reaching for his hand. I flipped it over, palm facing up, and rubbed a little of the oil on the inside of his wrists. When I was about to pull away, Aaron clasped my hand.

"Thank you," he said, looking directly into my eyes. "I feel better already. You must have a magic touch."

I laughed awkwardly. If he only knew.

As luck would have it, Fleur saved me from the moment by entering the room with a tray holding three cups of tea. Aaron released my hand on her arrival and shifted in his chair as she placed the tray on the table and took the seat on the sofa next to

Abby.

"Pwsss-Pwsss-Pswsss." Fleur patted her lap and Abby instantly honoured her by moving and curling up on it.

I handed Aaron a cup of tea and offered him sugar, which he declined, before taking up my own cup. "You must be amazing with animals," Aaron said to Fleur. "Abby's not a cat that normally takes to people."

"Abby, so that's your name," Fleur said while ruffling the cat's head. "She's a little sweetheart."

An idea began to form in my brain, but I decided to put a pin in it for now. Nothing could be done with the cat until I knew if anyone was coming to claim her. To my surprise, Niles also wandered in and jumped up on the arm of the chair next to me.

"And who's this handsome fellow?" Aaron asked.

"This is Niles, who is going to be on his best behaviour," I said, more for Niles than for anyone else.

"He's been in and out a few times," Fleur said. "I think he was making sure I was taking proper care of little Abby here."

"Hmm," I murmured, wondering what the rascal was up to. Although, maybe he'd sensed some magical ability in Fleur and had started thinking along the same lines as me.

We finished our tea and decided to head out to Cardiff to see Benjamin. I was a little concerned that it might be too soon to visit him. I hated to intrude on his grief, but Aaron echoed his belief that he might need a helping hand. Fleur agreed to continue watching the store and after Aaron told her about his near-miss with the chimney, she agreed to call the council and let them know about the hazard and danger.

~

It took us a good forty minutes in the bad M4 traffic before we reached Benjamin's place in Cardiff. I didn't know the area at all, but Aaron said it was a common place for students to live. The street comprised a row of terraced houses, all with bay-front windows and a small walled area in front where most of the residents kept their wheelie bins and recycling bins. It was nearing midday, and the sun shone overhead. I squinted in its brightness and shifted my bag onto my shoulder, glad that I had forgone a jacket in the heat.

Aaron directed me to number 153, which had an aged tourmaline blue door with the paint peeling away. I took a deep breath, unsure what would happen while Aaron knocked.

After a few minutes and some heavier banging on the door on Aaron's part, a young man who looked to be around the same age as Fleur answered the door. He looked a state. His T-shirt was crumpled and stained with what looked like both tea and a tomato-based sauce. His face had patches of a stringy beard covering it, and his dark hair was all over the place. But most notable of all were his dark and puffy eyes.

"How you holding up, Ben?" Aaron asked, reaching out his hand. Benjamin clasped onto it and shook his head. Aaron pulled him in for a hug. "I'm sorry to hear about your mum," he said. "I know the news is still recent and you might not be in the mood for visitors, but I thought it best to come and see if you needed anything."

Benjamin pulled away and wiped at his nose with the back of his hand. "Thanks, Aaron," he said. "Come in."

He turned and walked through the hallway and into a room on the right. Aaron waved for me to go first and followed behind us both, guiding me with his hand on the small of my back. I tried not to react to the over-familiar gesture and focused on my surroundings. The room Benjamin led us to was dark and dingy with what looked like a duvet cover over the windows in place of curtains. The furniture was worn and dated and had even more stains on it than Benjamin's top.

Benjamin flopped down in the seat nearest the TV in the corner and I perched on the edge of the sofa. Aaron joined me.

"This is Eira Snow," Aaron said, introducing me. "She discovered your mum last night."

"I'm very sorry for your loss," I said. "I appreciate this must be a very difficult time for you."

Benjamin grunted in response. "I called Aunty Trisha to let her know what happened. She is notifying everyone else. She also said she'd help with the funeral arrangement and get some information and figures together for me. But I don't know the first thing about any of that sort of stuff."

"Do you know if your mum had already made arrangements?" I asked, wondering if she'd secured a plot with her husband.

"She wouldn't share anything like that with me."

Aaron shifted beside me on the sofa. "It might be a good idea to go through her office and see if she has any paperwork. We'll have to notify the bank and cancel any policies she has. But don't worry," Aaron added, noting the disquieted look on Benjamin's face. "I can go through everything with you."

Benjamin cleared his throat and wiped at his nose again. I wished there was something I could do to help him. Although I'd been reluctant to consider him a suspect in his mother's murder, in the back of my mind, I had filed away the possibility. But looking at him now, at how broken-hearted and dejected he was, I couldn't imagine him being the guilty party.

"The last time I saw her, we fought," Benjamin said.

Aaron nodded. "Parents and kids fight all the time. And Lord knows your mum wasn't always the easiest person to get along with, especially following your father's death."

Benjamin stood and paced the room for a second, running his hand through his unkempt hair. "She could be so damn infuriating at times." He flung himself back on the seat. "I was never good enough for her. Could never do anything right." He cleared his throat and shook his head. "She said I was just like Dad. A waste of space. Like she didn't get everything she had from Dad. He was a million times a better person than she was."

"I have the same sort of relationship with my father," I said, not bothering to add that we hadn't spoken in more than ten years. "But I'm sure she loved you just as you loved her."

"I should call Susan Reynolds," Benjamin said. "She was Mum's best friend, but I haven't got her number. Aunt Trisha doesn't either."

"The number will be at your mum's in all likelihood," Aaron said. "Maybe you would feel better coming back to Caerleon with us and seeing what we can find."

"Yes," I agreed. "Sometimes it's better to keep busy and be doing things in situations like this."

Benjamin stood again and seemed to become aware of his appearance for the first time. He pulled his T-shirt away from his body and looked at it. "I should change first," he said before sniffing his armpits. "Shower too. Do you mind waiting?"

"It's no bother, mate," Aaron said just as a knock sounded on the front door.

Benjamin left, and we heard muffled voices before he returned to the front room. Detective Inspector Kate McIntyre followed behind him. The look that crossed her face when she entered was anything but pleased.

"Ms Snow," she said, turning her attention to me. "I believe in your statement last night you mentioned not knowing Mrs Smith. Why, therefore, am I finding you in the residence of her son today?"

I stood, not liking the way she tried to tower over me. "I simply came to offer my condolences and see if I could be of any help," I said. "Plus, if you remember, I do have Mrs Smith's cat and thought it best to let Benjamin know in case he wished to take her into his care."

Benjamin sat back down, scoffed, and scrunched his nose in disgust.

The DI backed away and took the only vacant seat on the other side of the room. With her no longer standing, I retook my perch. "I need to ask you a few questions," she said, and removed a pen and a pad from her pocket. "Which I would prefer to do alone."

Aaron shook his head. "And I would prefer to be here to support Benjamin should he need it," he said while Benjamin nodded in agreement. He didn't look at all comfortable in the detective's presence. His already rattled exterior had taken on a definite air of panic.

"And you are exactly?"

"Aaron Jenkins. Tanya Smith was my mother's neighbour. I've been a friend to Benjamin and his family for years."

"The neighbour you delivered your package to last night," she said, pointing her pen at me.

"That's correct. Samantha Jenkins," I confirmed.

Without acknowledging my answer, the detective turned her attention back to Benjamin. "It is my understanding that you argued with your mother within the last week. An argument that spilled onto the streets, as I've come to understand."

"Something he's not hiding," I said, not liking her tone. "He expressed regret at their argument being the last time they talked moments before you arrived."

"Indeed," she said. "So, you admit there was an argument. Would you mind telling me what it was in relation to?"

Benjamin clasped his hands together and sat forward in his chair. He pinched and rubbed at his finger, making it white from the obvious pressure he applied. "The same as always," he said.

"You fought often?"

His fidgeting increased, and I worried he might break his hand the way he was squeezing it. "She was never happy. Not with the way I dressed, the way I walked, the uni course I'd taken. Yeah, we fought often."

"You might say it's reasonable to assume you were mad at your mother?"

"I'm sorry," I interjected. "It was my understanding that you were treating Mrs Smith's death as an accident, but your line of questioning seems to imply that you consider Benjamin a suspect in her death."

"We need to look at all possibilities," the detective said, even though she had completely dismissed the idea that Tanya's death was anything other than an accident the night before.

Aaron stood. "Then I believe your questioning is over. If you would like to speak with Ben again, then you can do so only in the presence of his solicitor."

Kate McIntyre plastered a smile on her face and made a show of very slowly putting away her pen and pad. "That won't be necessary. For now."

She stood as if to leave, but Benjamin slammed his fist into the wall beside him, making me jump.

He growled and paced the room. "It would be typical of Mum to get herself murdered and for me to go down for it," he said. "One final kick to the gut. She'd like that."

"Benjamin," Aaron warned, but Benjamin's nostrils flared, and he punched the wall again.

The detective looked on, assessing. He wasn't doing himself any favours, letting his temper flare in front of her. Nor me either, for that matter, as I'd have to reassess his capacity for violence. I stood, feeling a little vulnerable, sitting in the face of his aggression.

"You know what," Benjamin said, clenching his fists. "If she got murdered, then she got everything she deserved." He turned his attention to me and almost spat in my face. "And that stupid cat. I hate that stupid cat. I'd have killed that spoilt creature too if I'd been the one to kill Mum."

I stepped forward into him, my own anger flaring. "Except she wasn't there, was she?" Benjamin looked taken aback for a second, but a look of complete rage soon replaced his momentary shock. He stared straight into my eyes, and despite my sympathy for his grief, I wanted to punch him right in the face. How could he say such a horrible thing about a poor, defenceless little animal? If he felt that way about Abby, maybe he did have it in him to kill his mother. "Abby was missing. You said earlier with quite some vehemence that your mother got everything she had from your father. Well, presumably with your mother now dead, that will all be coming to you," I said. "That might be considered a motive for murder. Isn't that right, Detective?"

I turned to see Kate smirking at me. Benjamin continued glaring at me, his anger reflecting my own. I almost wanted him to lash out at me. At least then, I'd know for certain what he was capable of.

Aaron cleared his throat. "Maybe it's best if you leave," he said and raised his eyebrows pointedly. "I'll meet you outside." He stepped forward and placed a hand on Benjamin's shoulder. "I'll take Eira back to Caerleon and come back for you," he said before turning to Kate. "Will it be okay for us to look through Tanya's papers and see if she has any funeral plans?"

"Not yet," Kate said. "I'd prefer you stay away from the house for now. I'll let you know when you can gain access." She huffed out a breath and her face took on a solemn look. "As soon as I get word your mother's body can be released, I'll let you know."

Benjamin nodded, and Kate motioned with her head for me to leave with her. I did.

"I don't want you meddling in this case," she said as soon as we were outside.

I crossed my arms in front of my chest and puffed myself up a little. "Yesterday, according to you, there was no case. What changed?"

"Nothing, officially. Yet," she added. "Let's just say, I'm not ready to dismiss your belief that this might, and I stress the word *might*, be a murder." I beamed and was about to say something when Kate raised her hand. "But what I said stands. I don't want you meddling in this case."

"Fine," I said, without highlighting the fact that Kate's definition of meddling may be vastly different from mine. Besides, now that she was looking at the possibility of murder, there should be no need for me to meddle. Although... "There is something you should know. It might be nothing, but when Aaron was walking in Caerleon, part of a derelict building fell and almost hit him. Doesn't that seem odd to you?"

Kate shook her head. "Don't start seeing killers everywhere," she said. "Sometimes things really are accidents."

I glanced back at the house. I could see the silhouettes of Aaron and Benjamin through the duvet cover hanging over the window. With the way their arms were moving, it didn't look like they were having a friendly conversation. "Will you question Benjamin again?" I asked.

"Not with your friend in the room." She huffed and eyed me with her curious dog-like head tilt. "I did some research on you," she said. A weight dropped into my stomach like an obsidian rock. "Your ex-husband is currently doing time for fraud."

"That has nothing to do with me. As you said, he's my ex."

"I just want to make sure you're not in the same line of work as he is."

I bristled. "Chris conned a lot of people, and I was at the very top of that list. I would never try to extort money from anyone. Least of all a grieving family."

"If you were trying," Kate said with a smirk on her face, "I'm not sure your display in there was the best way to go about it." She stepped closer. "Unless, of course, you have some evidence linking Benjamin to the murder and are laying the groundwork to blackmail him."

Aaron cleared his throat. Kate and I turned to see him watching us in the doorway. "Everything okay?" he asked.

"Everything's fine," I said.

"Yes," Kate agreed. "I'm just leaving." She pointed two fingers at her eyes before waving them at me in the universal sign to signify she'd be watching me.

I let out a deep breath and turned to Aaron. "Do you fancy stopping somewhere and grabbing a cup of coffee?" I asked. I didn't know how much Aaron had heard, but given how he had placed his trust in me, he deserved an explanation.

CHAPTER FIVE

We stopped at the service station on the motorway back to Newport. We'd been silent in the car, but when we sat with our drinks, Aaron looked at me expectantly.

"My ex wasn't a nice man, as it turns out," I said.

"My ex wasn't a nice woman, but I have a feeling yours was bad in a different way than mine."

I gave him a half-smile and shrugged. "I was young when I met him. Nineteen. He was funny and clever and embraced my little... quirks."

"Quirks?"

"Being into crystals and oils. All that sort of stuff," I said, while keeping my eyes fixed firmly on the table. Aaron may have been entitled to some truths. But my being a witch wasn't one of them. Not yet. "He thought it was kind of cool. I sell a lot of stuff online and Chris would travel around the country meeting with suppliers. He wasn't home a lot."

"An affair?" Aaron said and reached across the table to still my hand, which twisted an empty sugar packet into oblivion.

I looked into his eyes, and from the pain I saw inside, I guessed his wife had been unfaithful.

"Yes," I said. "Many. A woman in every port. Isn't that what they say about sailors?" I gave an incredulous laugh. "Chris had a woman in near enough every county he visited for work. But that's not the worst of it. He used my business to exploit vulnerable people. I have an excellent reputation. My remedies work. Chris used that reputation and pretended to be psychic. He charged people for fake readings and even exploited a family whose son had gone missing. He conned them out of everything they had. That was the case that landed him in trouble and made me realise what was happening."

"How so?" Aaron said, listening intently, something Chris had never done unless he was trying to wheedle some knowledge he could use out of me.

"I found a bank statement when going through his travel case for his dirty washing one time after he returned from a trip. The amount of money in there was ridiculous. I couldn't understand where he'd got it all. But worse still, Chris' name was on the account, but not our home address." I took a sip of tea and tried to compose myself before continuing. It felt strange to be saying everything out loud. I'd lived it, but this was different. Sometimes it's easier to live through things and then bury them deep inside.

"I followed the trail, you might say, took a trip for myself. That's where I found his first mistress. She knew all about his pathetic wife back at home and took great delight in laughing in my face. She was also more than happy to show me everything she had belonging to Chris. Anyway, long story short, the documents she allowed me so generously to see led me to what Chris was doing. As soon as I realised that he'd conned that poor family, I went to the police."

"Were they able to return their money?" Aaron asked.

I smiled. "They didn't have to. Chris used the same bank passwords for his secret account as he had for our joint account. I transferred every penny back to the family before calling the police. I'm sure some of the money also came from Chris' fake psychic readings, but I couldn't trace them so passed that onto the family too." I didn't think it necessary to add that I'd also cleared out our joint accounts and transferred our money into an account of my own. After all, all of Chris' dodgy money had gone into the secret account. The money from ours had been from my business, which Chris had more than benefited from over the years.

Aaron finished his coffee and looked down at the table. "And their son?" he asked, making my heart swell. He was such a nice, caring man. Why couldn't I have met someone like him all those years ago instead of falling for a jerk like Chris?

"He came home all on his own. Chris had them searching all over the place with the pretence he'd been abducted. He honestly believed the kid had to be dead, but as it turns out, he had simply run away. Problems with some bullying at school."

"So, Chris is what, in jail? And the two of you are now divorced."

"That pretty much sums it up. As soon as my divorce papers were through, I disposed of every last connection I had with Chris and moved to Caerleon. I wanted a fresh start somewhere no one knew what Chris had done." I huffed out a deep breath and took a swig of my tea, feeling strangely lighter.

Aaron had stayed attentive through my whole confession and hadn't shown the slightest bit of judgement against me. His hand had never left my own. Even though there were times I'd blamed myself for everything that had happened. I'd been so stupid to trust Chris. The police told me I'd done the right thing in coming to them, that con artists have a knack for getting people to trust them, but they didn't know I was a witch. They didn't know that Niles had hated Chris from the very start, and I should have trusted his instinct.

Speaking of trust... I pulled my hand away from Aaron. I'd only met him a few hours earlier, but I needed him to believe in me, even though I held my true nature back.

"I really believe that someone murdered Tanya," I said, and shook my head. If only her ghost had given me something to go on. For all I knew, she might not have been willing to accept her daft choice in footwear was responsible for her death and had chosen to declare it a murder to absolve herself of any responsibility. "But I might be wrong," I added. "If the past has taught me anything, it's that I may not be the best at noticing everything going on around me."

Aaron grabbed my hand again and squeezed. "I think you knew more than you gave yourself credit for. With my ex, I knew something was going on. I just chose to deny it. It's easier to block out the truth than admit your life has gone completely wrong."

I smiled and squeezed back. "Thank you."

Aaron pulled away and clapped his hands on the table. "As I am no longer going with Benjamin to his mum's place. How about we pay a visit to Trisha and see what she has to say? Although maybe you should try not to get so defensive of the cat this time. I'm not sure antagonising everyone is the right way to play this."

"I'll try," I said. Although, truth be told, if Tanya's sister in any way threatened Abby the way Benjamin had, I might not be able to stop myself.

~

Aaron called his mum again, who I was fast learning to be a fountain of information, and gained Trisha's address. They went to church together and, from the sounds of it, were quite close. She only lived down the road from Tanya, even though she was in the next village, and it was easy to find her home. A large bay-fronted semi-detached with red velvet curtains drawn open and displaying the living room in all its pristine glory.

Unlike the welcome we'd received from Benjamin, Trisha's welcome was warm and friendly. She thanked us for our kind visit and offered us some tea and biscuits. Not wanting to appear rude, we both accepted. I had to admit she wasn't quite what I was expecting from her sister. She wore black work trousers with penny-loafers and a long-sleeved top that looked a little too hot given the temperature. She was buttoned up as tight as a nun. The complete opposite of Tanya in her very short dress and impossibly high heels.

"We've just come from Ben's," Aaron said as we sat, and Trisha poured us both a bone-china cup of tea from a matching teapot.

"Milk and sugar?" she offered, and we both opted for just the milk.

"I spoke to him on the phone earlier and told him not to worry about calling everyone else. I'd take care of it." She said the words with a smile that suggested she'd done something saintly. "Of course," she added. "I couldn't have him knowing how many men I had to notify. A boy shouldn't have to face his mother's indiscretions after her death." She handed us both our cups and saucers and lifted hers to her mouth, taking the smallest sip possible before adding another spoon of sugar.

"Tanya enjoyed life," Aaron said, as if trying to justify her actions to me rather than Trisha. "I guess I can understand that after her husband passed."

Trisha pffted. "That's no excuse for the way she behaved, gallivanting around with goodness knows who, spending her money as if it grew on trees with never a thought of helping others. You, of all people, should know what she was like, having been one of her conquests. If your mother hadn't talked sense into you, I'd have likely been phoning you last night to save Benjamin the trouble as well. Not that you don't cause her enough grief with the way you behave."

She flashed Aaron a disapproving look, and I wondered what she was talking about.

Aaron cleared his throat and rested his saucer on his knee. "Yes, well. My relationship with Tanya was a long time ago, and as you said, over. As to anything else..."

"She had two on the hook at the moment? At least, that's all I knew about. I called Frank, and he was terribly upset. I honestly think he thought she might marry him someday. But there was no chance of that. I shouldn't speak ill of the dead—" I blinked back my confusion, thinking that's exactly what she'd already been doing for the last five minutes, "—but there was no chance of that. Tanya married for money the first time, and Frank is far from wealthy."

"And the other man?" I prompted, ignoring the disdain in her voice.

Trisha rolled her eyes and glanced around the living room as though assessing everything's worth and deciding it came up short. I followed her gaze and couldn't help but notice that while everything appeared expensive and well-made, there was also a slight fading to the colours of the curtains and rug, and some fraying at the edges. "David," she said after a moment, and cleared her throat as though saying the name pained her. "Unfortunately, I haven't been able to reach him yet. His phone keeps going through to voicemail and I haven't had the heart to leave a message. It's not the sort of thing you should hear in a recording. I managed to contact his work, though, and his business partner told me he's out of town on a business trip for a few days. Said he was likely in meetings." She shrugged and took another sip of tea. "I'll try again tonight after office hours."

I mirrored her actions and took a sip of my own tea, wondering how any woman could juggle two men at the same time. Then I remembered Chris had managed far more than two women and hadn't seemed to have any problems. It all just felt like far too much work for me.

"Pardon me for asking," I said, brushing one of Abby's white hairs from my lap, "but did the two men, Frank and David, know about each other?"

"I would assume so," Trisha said, letting out an exasperated sigh. "No doubt, they were as bad as Tanya and had other women on the side too," she added, although I wondered how true that could be when she'd mentioned Frank holding out the hope of marriage. When I said as much, she agreed. Frank might not have. "He was never happy with her seeing David. I can tell you that much. He didn't like the way David treated her, showing up out of the blue a couple of times a year and vanishing again. Tanya dropped everyone and everything when David was around. So, you're probably right."

As soon as we'd finished our tea, Trisha thanked us for our well wishes and for calling in to see her, but said that she had to go to town on some errands. Knowing a polite cue to leave when we heard one, we thanked her for the tea and stood to leave.

The front door opened as we reached it and a stressed-looking man in a rumpled suit entered. He stood straighter and composed himself when he noticed me and Aaron.

"Everything okay, dear," Trisha said, moving to greet him and placing a kiss on his cheek. He gave her a half smile and nodded. "This is Aaron. You remember? Samantha's boy."

"Ahh, yes," said the man, who reached his hand out and shook Aaron's hand.

"And this is Eira Snow. She's new to the village and found poor Tanya's body last night."

"Terrible tragedy," he said and shook my hand, too.

"They're just leaving," Trisha said and ushered us out the front door.

Although no introduction to the man was offered, Aaron confirmed my assumption that he was Trisha's husband when the door closed behind us.

I followed him out onto the street, where he stopped outside the gate and ran his hand over his head as though he was thinking. "There is one more person we should probably speak to as we're doing the rounds," he said.

"Who?"

"Susan Reynolds."

"Benjamin mentioned she was Tanya's best friend."

"She was probably closer to Tanya than either Trisha or Benjamin. They shared everything. If there's anyone who might give us a better idea about what was going on in Tanya's life, it would be Susan."

I nodded and glanced along the street in the same direction Aaron was looking. The traffic was building, so I looked at my watch and noted it to be 12:45 p.m. No doubt, people were running errands on their lunch break. Normally, my tummy would have told me it was lunchtime by now, but given that I'd had a second breakfast and had drunk more tea already this morning than I would in a week, I guessed hunger was a long way from coming.

"Do you know where she lives?" I asked.

"Yep," Aaron confirmed and started walking back to his car, which we'd parked further along the road.

"Thank you for doing all this with me," I said as soon as he started the engine.

"Not a problem. It was right for me to pay my respects anyway, and if Tanya was murdered, I'd like to know who did it as much as you do. Probably more," he added with a touch of sadness in his voice.

It was then that I realised how thoughtless I'd been. Aaron had known Tanya for years. They'd even had a relationship, which, if Trisha was to be believed, only ended because

Samantha persuaded her son it was a bad idea. He must have some very conflicting feelings about everything that was happening. I didn't like to pry, but for all I knew, he might even have loved Tanya. He certainly seemed close to her son.

As we drove to Susan's house, I pondered everything we'd learned. It wasn't much. Benjamin was an angry young man who had a love-hate relationship with his mother and very much hated her cat. Though given Tanya's unfinished business was making sure her cat was okay and not her son, maybe he had his reasons for that. Then there was Trisha. She clearly disapproved of the way Tanya lived her life, and the way she mentioned her sister marrying for money had me wondering if she might have harboured a little jealousy towards her sister. I honestly wouldn't have put it past either one of them being Tanya's killer, but then there was also Frank and David to consider. David might have an alibi being out of town, but Frank, not so much. Although, we'd have to ask him, of course.

I sighed and rubbed at my temple.

"Anything wrong?" Aaron asked.

"I just realised that we never asked Benjamin or Trisha where they were last night."

Aaron smiled. "Don't you think that would have been rude?" he said.

"You make a good point." Detective Inspector Kate McIntyre

was right, I was no Ms Marple. I bet she could have wheedled the question into the conversation without antagonising anyone. I never was particularly good at being subtle. "I forgot to mention that I have Abby too," I said, remembering the white cat hair I'd found on my leg.

"We can do that another time, but I doubt she'd want the cat. Susan might be your best bet there," he said and pulled to the side of the road. "Speaking of which."

He motioned to the large house we were parked in front of and switched off the engine. I took a deep breath and followed him from the car.

As Aaron had said, Susan Reynolds proved to be the most affected by grief out of everyone we'd spoken to that day. She answered the door in her dressing gown and had done nothing to hide the fact that she was crying.

She ushered us inside after hugging Aaron, and in turn, me, and broke down with a fresh batch of tears. As Aaron knew her better than I did, I left her comforting to him. It took about ten minutes of her head buried against his chest for her to regain some composure.

"I'm very sorry we've intruded on you at this difficult time," I said.

"Don't be. I'm honestly glad someone thought of me. Trisha was very blunt in her call this morning and, although it sounds silly, she made me feel that as I wasn't family, I wasn't allowed to grieve along with her and Benjamin."

"Families are not all made of blood," I said, and Susan started crying again.

"I loved her so much," she said, while wiping the end of her nose with the back of her hand. "She was everything I had. I honestly don't know what I'm going to do without her."

The poor woman spluttered and broke out in a fresh batch of tears, flushing her already flustered face with the colour of rose quartz. Fitting when you think about it. The rose quartz is the stone of the heart, a crystal of unconditional love. I vowed to make her up some magical oil to ease her grief when I got home and deliver it as soon as possible.

"This must be how Tanya felt when Julie passed," Susan said as soon as her tears subsided.

My ears pricked, but I tried not to show any outward sign that I'd heard of Julie before. It would be extremely hard to explain how she'd come to collect Tanya's spirit and take her to the other side.

"Julie?" Aaron asked, sparing me the need.

Susan pulled away from him for the first time and straightened her dressing gown. "It doesn't matter," she said. "Julie was someone Tanya knew who died an awfully long time ago. I don't think she ever fully recovered following her death."

I nodded in understanding. It certainly seemed as though Tanya and Julie had a close relationship. It was only then I questioned why she had come for Tanya instead of Tanya's husband. But then I remembered Trisha saying she'd married for money. Benjamin may also have insinuated the same thing when he said everything she had was thanks to his father. If their marriage wasn't built on love, why should he come?

"Grieving can be a very difficult process and if there is anything I can do to help, please let me know," I said. "I have some oil that will do you wonders and help you get some rest. I'll pop it over later."

"You are too kind. Tanya would have liked you." She looked at me for a second and her mouth opened and closed as though she wanted to ask me something. I smiled and hoped she would see it as encouraging. "Did she look as though she suffered?" Susan asked after a moment.

"No. I don't think she did." I didn't feel the need to add that, from the angle of her neck, death would have been instantaneous.

"Still, she suffered these past few days anyway," Susan added. "Her poor cat Abby was catnapped—"

"Catnapped?"

"Yes. Abby would never run away. Tanya was convinced someone had been in her house and snatched her. She was worried sick. She loves... loved that cat more than life itself. I do hope she's safe somewhere."

"Then let me put your mind at ease on that, at least. Abby is safe and well at my place. I found her last night when she returned home. I was wondering if you would like her. She might be a help to you during this difficult time."

Susan shook her head. "I'm allergic, I'm afraid. Abby has no one to look after her."

"Benjamin doesn't want her," Aaron noted. "But we forgot to mention her to Trisha."

Susan scoffed. "Trisha hates that cat as much as Benjamin does. More so, probably, and the feeling was mutual. Abby would likely scratch her eyes out if Trisha came near her." Susan stood and walked over to a sideboard and opened her drawer. "That reminds me," she said. "Tanya had placed a reward for whoever found the cat. That should go to you."

I stood. "Absolutely not. I couldn't possibly consider taking a penny of the money."

"No, I promised Tanya I would pay ten thousand pounds to whoever rescued Abby, and that's you. I intend to honour that commitment."

"No. I insist. Even if you write me that cheque," I said, watching as she did just that. "I wouldn't cash it."

Susan's shoulders sagged, and she stilled her hand. "I said

Tanya would have liked you. Just promise that you'll make sure Abby finds a good home if you can't keep her yourself," she said.

"I promise."

Aaron stood and walked to my side. "We should probably get going," he said. "Susan, if you need anything, give me a call." He pulled a business card from his pocket and handed it to her.

I was about to say goodbye when something she'd said struck me. "If you don't mind me asking, why did you agree to pay the reward money for Abby? Couldn't Tanya pay it herself?"

"Oh goodness me, no. Tanya was flat broke."

"Didn't she inherit a lot of money from Phill?" Aaron asked.

"She burnt through that eons ago. You know how she liked to spend."

CHAPTER SIX

We arrived back at the shop after Susan's house, and despite it only being around four in the afternoon, I was completely shattered.

Fleur confirmed the shop had been quiet, and we sat down to yet another cup of tea.

"Do you really think that Abby was catnapped?" Fleur asked after we ran through everything we'd heard.

I shrugged. "If she was, why was she suddenly back?"

Susan would have said if she'd paid out any ransom money. Unless, of course, she only tried to pay me as a cover. I shook my head. That didn't make any sense; besides, she was truly grief-stricken. I hated myself for doubting everyone.

"That's another question to add to the pile," Aaron said.

Fleur pulled her phone out and looked at the time. "Is it okay if I call it a day?" she asked. "I need to be somewhere."

"Of course," I said. I'd really taken advantage of her generosity today. Aaron's too. "If you come by in the morning, we can discuss wages and everything." Fleur's face beamed at this, making me worry she might be a bit cash-strapped now. I stood, walked over to the till, and pulled out a hundred pounds. "Take this for now, and we'll talk in the morning," I said again.

"Wow, really? Thanks."

Aaron sat forward as soon as she left and laughed.

"What's so funny?" I asked.

He stood and walked close to me, taking my hands. "Today has been the strangest date I've ever been on," he said.

My stomach flip-flopped. "Date? I'm not sure that's what I'd call it. But then again, the dating world has changed a considerable amount since my last one."

He brushed an errant hair from my face, the back of his hand lingering on my cheek. "It started with me asking you out for breakfast. That makes it a date. Plus, of course, we said we'd go for dinner tonight."

I didn't want to spoil the moment, but asked if he'd mind taking a rain check. I really was exhausted and still wanted to make something to help Susan. "We could always do it tomorrow night," I suggested.

"How about we meet again for breakfast?" he countered. "We still have some sleuthing to do."

This time, I laughed. "Sleuthing. Sounds like a plan."

"Then it's a second date," he said and leaned forward, brushing his lips against my own, sealing them in the best kiss I'd had in twenty years.

"I'll see you in the morning," he said, pulling away.

"In the morning," I agreed and followed him to the door. I stood there for a few minutes watching him leave and wondering how right he had been. Date or otherwise. Today could easily be among my top ten strangest. Ever since I found Tanya's body, I'd felt like I'd been on a rollercoaster full of ups and downs. And I could definitely say that Aaron was one of the highlights.

Niles let out a quick mew behind me and I turned to pet him on the head. "Hungry?" I asked, noting how Abby came up behind him. I had no idea what had happened between them during the day, but they seemed to have come to an understanding. "Come on, you two, let's see what we can scrounge up for food, and then you can help me work a spell for a nice lady I met today. Abby," I added. "We also need to have a conversation regarding your future. Niles can show you the ropes and you can let us know how you feel."

With that, I turned the sign on the door to 'closed', switched off the lights, and headed back to the cottage with the two cats in tow.

CHAPTER SEVEN

Aaron entered the shop the next morning to find me and Fleur going through the inventory and discussing the properties of each item.

I smiled at seeing his friendly face, but had to admit I was somewhat shocked when he came over and gave me a peck on the cheek in greeting. A flush of warmth flooded my cheeks and Fleur raised her eyebrows in question at me. We hadn't discussed my divorce and the events that preceded it, yet, but she knew I'd been married for a long time before moving to Caerleon.

"You ready for the day ahead?" Aaron asked. "I took the liberty of calling Trisha and gaining the contact details for Frank and David."

"I'm surprised she gave them to you," I said, trying to ignore the fluttering in my stomach from his over-familiar greeting, and the way his sweet, woody scent washed over my senses.

Aaron winked and smiled. "I used my wit and charm," he said, and Fleur spluttered back a laugh.

"I'm sure you did," she said, and I gave her a pointed look.

Aaron saw the humour in her comment and chuckled to himself before saying that he'd told her he was helping Ben with the funeral.

"She was a bit reluctant, and insisted she had the arrangements in hand. From her tone, I'd say she wanted to be in control of everything. But after a little reassurance that Ben was happy to leave all the details to her, she relented. She still hasn't been able to reach David," he added. "But I gave Frank a call before coming here and asked if it was okay for us to pop in to see him around lunchtime."

"And he was okay with that? I mean, he wasn't curious why?"

Aaron walked over to the table and grabbed a sherbet lemon from the bowl. "He was fine. We, ugh—" he ran his hand through his hair, "—we actually met a few years back, so the conversation wasn't as awkward as you might imagine. Tanya was dating Frank at the same time she and I were together."

Fleur looked as though she was about to explode with questions, but I silenced her with a slight shake of my head. Aaron had been completely upfront about his relationship with Tanya, and it had to be hard for him to help me find her killer. If there even was one. He didn't need a million questions from Fleur on the subject. Not when, in truth, it was neither her business nor mine.

"Right," Aaron said, popping the sweet in his mouth. "I'm starving. How about we grab that breakfast?"

I smiled. I'd held off eating this morning as he said we'd be eating out again, and my stomach had reminded me it was empty with low growls for the last half an hour.

"I'll be fine here for the day." Fleur smirked. I could tell she thought the budding relationship I had with Aaron was kind of cute. Some might find it condescending coming from a teenager, given all the life experience I had. But I was the first to admit, in starting a new relationship, Fleur probably had way more experience than I did. Sheesh, she wasn't even born the last time I'd had a first... or second date.

I was about to grab my bag when the front door slammed open. The bell ripped from its mooring and fell to the ground with a deafening clatter.

"Why are you hell-bent on causing me trouble?" Benjamin screamed while storming into the store. His face was flushed, and his hair unkempt as the day before. He lashed out and kicked the coffee table, sending the flowers and sherbet lemons scattering all over the floor.

"Benjamin," Aaron said, his voice a low warning growl. "What do you think you're doing?"

Benjamin stormed toward me with rage plastered all over his face. Instinctively, I raised my hand, ready to use a spell to blast him away should the need arise. Thankfully, Aaron saved me from unleashing my magic and revealing my secret by stepping between us and placing a hand on Benjamin's chest to hold him back.

Benjamin looked down at the hand, his nostrils flaring. "What am I doing? What is she *bleeping* doing? That policewoman called me this morning. She wants a formal interview and suggested I call a solicitor. I couldn't understand why. When she called and told me mum had been found, she said it was an accident, but then..." he scowled at me over Aaron's shoulder and edged forward. Aaron pushed him back. "It's all because of you," he almost spat. "I bet you killed my mum. What were you doing in her *bleeping* house, anyway?"

"Benjamin." Aaron's voice took on a hard edge, and he grabbed the younger man by the arm and pulled him towards the door. "I think you need to leave. Eira is just doing what she thinks is right. Now, I don't think you killed your mum, but if you keep acting this way, the police sure as hell will. Have you called a lawyer yet?"

"I shouldn't *bleeping* need a lawyer!" He yanked his arm from Aaron's and swung it around, slamming it into the shelving nearest him. The bottles and crystals smashed on the floor. The scent that filled the air could clear the nostrils of an elephant. Benjamin had easily caused several thousand pounds' worth of damage in one blow.

Aaron got rougher with him this time, opened the front door, and pushed him onto the street outside.

"Drama!" Fleur said as I silently watched Aaron shove Benjamin.

Benjamin shoved him back, but whatever Aaron said soon had the fight leaving him. As soon as his anger subsided, he stood, shoulders slumped like a defeated child.

"We'd better get all of this cleaned up," Fleur said after a moment. I waited for a second, still watching as Aaron led Benjamin away from the shop.

"I'll grab the dustpan and brush from the kitchen. We'll need the mop too." I turned to see Niles staring at me. He looked as though he'd half considered transforming. "You and me both," I said, glad that we'd resisted our natural instincts and kept from exposing ourselves.

I returned a minute later and set to work cleaning all the

broken shards from the floor. Fleur held open a black bag, and we both had the mess cleaned away in no time. I was just grateful none of the oils had made it to the rug, otherwise I'd be shopping for a new one.

"We'll have to fix the shelf and get some new stock made up to fill it." Despite everything, I turned to Fleur and smiled. "It looks like you'll be learning some magic spells sooner than you thought," I said. "How does spending this evening in the workshop sound?" I'd need all the help I could get to replace everything Benjamin had destroyed.

Fleur gave me a tentative smile, and I noticed a worried flicker in her eyes.

I patted her on the shoulder. "Don't worry, we'll take it slow."

She huffed out her breath and scrunched up her nose. "It's not that," she said. "I just don't have a lot of time this evening. You could say I'm between living arrangements. I was sleeping on a friend's sofa, but her boyfriend just moved in and things are a little awkward. I need to spend some time looking for a place to live."

"That's easy. I mean, if you'll consider it, there's a place upstairs. It's only a one-bed flat, but it's furnished and has a pleasant sitting room and a kitchen big enough to fit a breakfast table in."

Fleur practically bounced on the spot. Her face lit up and

when she spoke, she sounded almost giddy. "Are you serious?" she asked before sobering. "I don't have a lot of money. How much is the rent? I'm not sure I'll be able to afford it."

I smiled. "As long as you're willing to work hard, I don't see that being much of a problem. Why don't you go take a look and see if it's any good to you?"

Fleur gathered me into a great big hug before I gave her the key to upstairs and she ran off to check out what I had no doubt would be her new home, at least for a while. I could scrub finding a tenant off my to-do list.

I finished straightening the store by tossing out the lemon drops, which had been spilt over the floor, and opening a new packet. Luckily, the bowl hadn't smashed, and neither had the vase, which I popped the flowers back in. They looked a little less perky than they had, but still had plenty of life left in them yet.

My stomach rumbled, once again reminding me that I hadn't eaten. I glanced outside, thinking wistfully of breakfast, and noted Samantha heading towards the store through the window.

"I've just seen Aaron and Benjamin," she said, removing her jacket and tossing it over the back of the chair. I was pleased to see no trace of her puffy eyes remained, and the peppermint and eucalyptus oil I'd spelled to help with allergies had worked. Not that I ever doubted it would. "I've left them at my place to sort out a solicitor. Aaron asked me to pop over and tell you he's the one that will have to take a rain-check today. He'll come and see you later if he can." Samantha looked at the space that yesterday held some shelves and products, sat on the sofa, and tutted. "He always was hot-headed, that boy. It's no surprise given the way his mother acted after his father died."

I offered Samantha a cup of tea. Her face was stern, but she sat and looked set to accept when Fleur came back into the store, gushing about how amazing the flat was. Abby followed behind her. At first, Abby eyed Samantha warily, but she edged closer. Samantha reached her hand out towards her and allowed her to sniff it for a few seconds before rubbing her on the head.

Realising that they hadn't met before, I introduced Fleur and Samantha. Fleur smiled warmly, but Samantha only gave a slight nod of her head before standing.

"I've no time to stop," she said, her tone abrupt. "I'm just here to relay Aaron's message."

With that, she turned to leave, but stopped when I called her back. "Your jacket," I said, gathering it from the back of the chair and handing it to her. It held Aaron's sweet, woody scent, and made me worry that the altercation with Benjamin had derailed whatever we had going on. I could understand Aaron staying with Benjamin to calm him down and help him arrange a solicitor, but would that really take all day? And what about

Frank? Would we be able to catch up with him later or was my investigation, such as it was, at a standstill for today? I debated asking Samantha if she knew anything about him, but the look on her face stalled my questions.

She snatched the jacket from my hand and stormed back towards the exit. I gave Fleur a confused shrug. Samantha froze by the door and turned to face me.

"I wasn't sure whether or not to say anything," she said, making my stomach turn to rock. "But I think I will. It's a disgrace that you're spreading rumours about Tanya being murdered."

"I'd hardly say I was spreading rumours. I only voiced my concerns to Aaron and the police—"

She held her hand up to stop me from talking.

"Disgraceful gossip," she said, her nose firmly in the air. "I really thought you were a more upstanding person than that." Her gaze flickered to Fleur and a look of disgust washed over her face. "But now I see the sort of company you keep—"

"Excuse me?" I fumed.

"No. I don't think I will. I'll be telling Aaron to stay away from you. You're just as much trouble as Tanya was to her poor family. That silly boy, too. If she was murdered, which I believe to be nothing more than your overactive imagination, then she deserved everything she got."

"Well, *Mrs Jenkins*. I actually thought you were a more upstanding person than you clearly are. I think it's best you leave."

She shot her nose even further in the air and stormed through the door.

"Nice woman, Aaron's mum," Fleur said.

"I'm so sorry she looked at you like that. She was so nice the other day." Once again, I'd proved what an awful judge of character I was.

Fleur shrugged and smiled. "Racism can't help but bubble to the top in some people. I'm used to it."

"Well, you shouldn't be... I mean, you shouldn't have to experience it once, let alone that many times you become used to it." To top off my words, my stomach decided it was time to loudly protest the fact that I still hadn't fed it.

Fleur laughed, and I suggested we close for a few hours and go grab some food at the café.

As we were closing shop, I noticed a council van and a couple of men at the derelict building down the road. "Do you mind if we just check in over there?" I asked Fleur, nodding to the workers.

"Not at all," she said.

We crossed the road, and I called out to one of the men who was clearing away the fallen bricks. "Hello," I said, noting the cones and danger signs he was putting up around the scaffolding. "We're the people who called the council. I was here yesterday with a friend when part of the chimney fell, almost hitting him."

The worker huffed out a sigh and turned to face me with a scowl, clearly expecting some sort of reprimand. I almost felt guilty speaking to him, but it wasn't my fault if other people used him as a soundboard for all their frustrations.

"There's no issue," I said, raising my hands in a low surrender position to try to placate him. "I just wondered if you know why it happened. I mean, I know the building needs work, but I wouldn't have thought it was bad enough to send bricks raining down on people's heads."

He rubbed the back of his neck and looked up at the roof. "You're right there," he said. "It looks safe enough inside, but given the circumstances, we need to get a surveyor out for a proper inspection before we can safely make our way up top and figure out what happened. We're just here to warn people away for now."

"Ah, I see." I followed his gaze, straining my neck to try to see anything out of place. "Do you know how long that will take?"

"We'll be back Monday afternoon."

"Okay. Thank you for your time," I said.

He nodded to me and Fleur, and we crossed back over the

road towards the café.

I couldn't get the incident out of my head for some reason. It might have been silly, and I was sure Detective Inspector Kate McIntyre was one hundred percent correct. Some accidents were just that, but that didn't mean this was.

I racked my brain trying to pinpoint what it was that bugged me most about the derelict house, and I kept coming back to Mrs Jenkins — I'd resolved never to call her Samantha again — and her vehemence, not just towards me and Fleur, but also to Tanya. Mrs Jenkins and Benjamin both said that Tanya deserved whatever she got, even murder. And Aaron mentioned Tanya as someone he could envision being murdered. That's not really a normal reaction to have when someone dies. If someone was angry with Tanya and the way she consorted with men, angry enough to kill her, then would they also be angry with the men she dated? Aaron could count himself on that list, and Trisha still hadn't managed to reach David. There's no knowing what could have happened to him. Then there was Frank. Trisha mentioned him holding out hope of Tanya marrying him. Maybe he'd finally realised that was never going to happen and snapped.

"Eira... Eira." Fleur nudged my elbow. "Are you coming in?"

I blinked and realised that she was holding the door to the café open for me to enter. I must have frozen in thought. "Sorry,"

I said. "I was miles away."

Fleur smiled. "I noticed. Anything important?"

I glanced back at the building. The workmen were pulling away. The man we'd spoken to saw me looking and nodded his head in goodbye. "They said it was Monday, they'd be back, didn't they?" I asked.

"Yeah, Monday afternoon."

"Perfect. Now that you're not busy tonight, what do you feel about a little trespass?"

Fleur followed my gaze to the derelict building. "What do you hope to find?" she asked.

"An answer."

CHAPTER EIGHT

The afternoon went by quickly. I helped Fleur settle her belongings into the flat. I'd honestly never seen anyone so grateful for such a small thing. You'd think I was setting her up in a mansion, complete with a swimming pool and tennis court. After that, she helped me process my online orders for the day and took them to the post office.

"Okay," I said when she returned. "Let's lock up, feed the cats, and get ready. We'll go as soon as it's dark."

Fleur straightened her back and thrust her chest out as though standing to attention. As always, her pixie cut was perfectly styled with not a hair out of place. But even with her smoky eyes, accentuated with black eyeliner and eyeshadow with a golden hue, she looked young in her tight ribbed sweater, black opaque tights, and denim shorts.

Looking at her, eager to learn and please, I couldn't help but wonder about her family. I knew she had a friend who'd let her sleep on her couch for a while. I also knew she had it in her to be a great witch. Anyone untrained who can use the power of their mind to move an object could do so much more with learning. But other than that, I didn't know the first thing about her. I'd been so wrapped up in everything I had going on that I hadn't given Fleur's circumstances a first, let alone a second, thought. I resolved to learn all I could about my apprentice, and given what we were about to do, my partner in crime.

"There are two stones we'll use tonight," I said as we walked through the garden towards my cottage. "Azurite and Iolite. Do you remember anything about them from your reading?" I asked.

"Azurite was called the Stone of Heaven by the ancient Chinese," she said. "And if I remember correctly, Iolite helps with psychic vision." She skipped a little and turned to face me. "Are you psychic?" she asked, her voice brimming with hopefulness.

I hated to burst her bubble, but confessed that wasn't a gift I possessed. In fact, I'd never actually met a true psychic. The thought made me think of Chris again and all that he'd done to hurt people. I wished I could send out a warning to everyone, never to trust a psychic. I'd thought about it a time or two. A simple disclaimer on my site. But that seemed hypocritical in some way. There were people who swore magic wasn't real, but I knew it was. Just because I'd never met a real psychic, that didn't mean they didn't exist.

I sighed and pushed open the door to the cottage. Abby and Niles darted through in front of us, ran into the kitchen, and jumped on the counter. "I think they're hungry," I said.

"I'll feed them. Where do you keep the food?"

"In the cupboard to the right of the sink," I said and flicked the kettle on while Fleur dealt with the cats. "Azurite," I continued, "is also said to help with psychic awareness. It enhances the inner vision, helps with making connections. Iolite serves as a bridge between the rational mind and the non-rational energies all around us."

"Non-rational energies?" she asked while shooing Niles away from Abby's bowl.

"Things like your heart and soul."

"Oh, okay." She furrowed her brows, and a look of confusion flashed over her face. "But if you're not psychic," she said after a moment, "what can you do with these stones that will help?"

The kettle clicked, and I grabbed two mugs from the cupboard while trying to think about how I could explain what

I was going to do to Fleur. "You've heard of an aura," I said after a moment. "It's basically the energy that someone emits. If someone stays in one place for a period of time, then that energy can linger for a while after they've gone."

Fleur's face lit up. "You're hoping to find a trace of the murderer's aura on the roof," she said.

I raised my hand to stop her thoughts from running away with themselves. In essence, I was hoping just that, but it also wasn't as simple as that.

"I'm hoping to find out if someone was on the roof. We know the council workmen haven't been up there yet. If we do find a trace, it could mean that the bricks that almost hit Aaron were pushed deliberately, but—"

"But it could also be a huge coincidence. Even if you find an aura, that doesn't mean that the person was there at the same time that you and Aaron were walking by. Even if they were, it could have been an accident. They could have nudged the bricks in passing and not even known Aaron was below."

"Exactly."

Fleur grabbed an apple from the fruit bowl on the counter and took a bite. "I thought you said you were after an answer," she said, pointing at me with the bitten apple in her hand.

"And if there's an aura, I'll get one."

Fleur shook her head and chuckled. "Yeah, as well as a billion more questions."

~

Getting into the building proved easier than expected. Fleur and I pretended to be looking at the flyers on the wall while checking the boarded fence for a way in. As luck would have it, the workmen had left a small gap we could squeeze through. We waited for a group of lads in the beer garden of the nearest pub to go back inside after their cigarette break and slipped in.

Shielded by the fencing, I glanced overhead at the scaffolding. We had to go up, but my stomach swirled, and my mind felt woozy. I gulped and looked around the outside.

"We'll have to go inside the house," I said, upgrading our trespass to breaking and entering.

The door was locked, but the wooden frame surrounding it was rotten and split with a few hard shoves. We stepped into complete darkness. All the windows were , and no glow from the sky or streetlights worked its way inside. Fleur clutched my hand and squeezed. I squeezed back, wondering why on Earth I wasn't heeding the detective's advice and refraining from meddling.

"Our eyes will adjust in a moment," I said. The smart thing to do would be to go home and grab a torch, but I worried my nerve would fail, and I wouldn't want to venture back out. "We'll stay still until we can make out any hazards and then move."

After a few moments, I saw the place was completely bare. Everything looked safe enough, and the outline of the stairs beckoned.

"Over there," Fleur said, as she spotted the same thing I had. "Let's head up."

I held tighter onto her hand and led the way through the dark house. I jumped at the slightest creak of the floorboards, and the wind that seemed slight outside howled through the cracks in the boards like a banshee.

"You don't think this place is haunted, do you?" Fleur asked, as she squealed and jumped after almost tripping over her own feet.

"Thanks for slotting that idea into my brain," I said. And then I remembered how little I'd actually shared with Fleur. We really needed to spend some time and get to know each other. "I meant to tell you why I thought Tanya's death was a murder." I took a deep breath. "She told me."

"She told you!" Fleur's voice came out as a strange sort of strangled shriek.

"Yes. Her ghost was there for a short while. She was very insistent on the matter and asked me to tell the police."

Fleur shuddered. "I was only kidding when I asked if this place might be haunted," she said. "Now I know ghosts are real, I'll be jumping at my own shadow."

"Don't be silly," I said, smiling. "You need light to create a shadow. It's far too dark for that in here."

"Ha-ha, very funny."

"Come on. We need to see if there's a way into the attic and onto the roof. Failing that, we'll have to climb outside onto the scaffolding and make our way up from there," I said, trying to make my voice more confident than I felt.

"You really do lead an interesting life," Fleur said.

"Not usually," I countered and dragged her with me to the foot of the stairs.

We stuck close to the walls. Fleur darted wide-eyed looks about her. She seemed half afraid of stumbling into a ghost and half excited by the prospect. Our feet clattered on the bare flooring and dust motes drifted in the air, shimmering in the meagre light that struck it.

After searching the upper floor for five minutes, I resolved myself to the idea of having to leave the relative safety of the house and venturing outside. I stood at the open window and sucked in a deep breath, bracing myself.

"Are you okay?" Fleur asked when I stalled on the ledge. "You've gone a little pale."

I pushed down the stark, screaming terror that threatened to bubble to the surface and nodded my head. "Let's get this over with."

Fleur pushed out onto the scaffolding first, and held her hand out to me, encouraging me to follow. I grabbed onto her as though my life depended on it. I had no doubt in my mind that it quite possibly did.

"It's not that bad," Fleur said.

"Yeah, for a sprightly nineteen-year-old," I countered.

Fleur rolled her eyes. "You're not that old," she said. "Come on, the way up is over here." I followed the direction of Fleur's nod and spotted the flimsy ladder going upwards. "You go first, and I'll follow behind you."

Great. I felt like a small child she was making sure was careful not to fall. Still, I was grateful for the gesture. I gripped the metal bars tight and edged towards the ladder at a snail's pace.

My throat , and it became hard to swallow. "It's very windy," I said, moistening my lips. "Do you think there's a chance we'll blow off?"

"It's not that windy," Fleur said. "Why did you decide to do this when you're clearly scared of heights?"

"I am not scared of heights." I am. Going as far as to say I'm terrified of heights would be an understatement. My stomach churned just thinking about where I stood. It took every ounce of strength I possessed not to lose my dinner to the idea of climbing to the roof.

"Don't witches fly on roomsticks?" she asked, as if the idea had suddenly dawned on her.

"Contrary to myths and legends, witches do not fly on broomsticks or on anything else, for that matter. At least, none I've ever heard of."

Fleur's gaze flashed to the roof. "It would be so much easier if they did."

I nodded in agreement. Instantly regretting the dizzying effect the motion had on my head. The wind whipped my hair into my face. I hooked it behind my ear and stepped onto the ladder. The time it took to reach the flat roof seemed like an age. As soon as I'd flipped myself over the ledge, I fell onto my back and closed my eyes. My heart pounded.

"Are you going to be able to get back down?" Fleur asked when she joined me.

I grumbled. I hadn't thought that far ahead. "We'll cross that bridge when we come to it," I said, and sat up before pulling the stones from my pocket. "Okay." I edged along the roof until I saw the spot the bricks must have fallen from. "We'll stop here so as not to taint the scene."

"What do we need to do?" Fleur asked.

I nodded to a stack of bricks a few feet away from the edge. "The bricks must have come from that pile," I said.

"Then there's no way they went over by accident. They're

way too far from the edge."

"I agree. But let's check for an aura anyway, just to be certain." I placed the Azurite stone in one hand and the Iolite in the other and asked Fleur to put her hands on top of them. "I can work the spell alone," I said. "But if you focus your mind on exploring the energy created and enhancing it, it will help you learn the feel of the spell."

Fleur nodded, and I focused on the energy humans gave off by their presence. Every molecule emits energy. I just needed to find the bit they left behind. I focused my mind, drifted a lazy gaze at the space on the roof by the bricks, and breathed in through my nose and out through my mouth, being sure to stay relaxed. Focusing my eyes too hard would keep the present image forefront in my mind and block any vision.

Magic swirled around us. Fleur gasped. She could feel the energy the same way I did. A tapestry of magical energy that overlaid anything, swaying like a gentle wave. After a moment, a fuzzy white light appeared as a ball beside us. It strengthened and grew, coalescing into a form. Fleur gaped at it wide-eyed.

"Do you see that?" she asked.

"Don't focus on how it looks. Tell me how it feels."

"It feels..." She closed her eyes. "It feels angry." At her words, the white shifted colour and turned a blazing red.

"Anything else?"

"It doesn't have a body so, is it silly to say that it feels kind of small? Like it doesn't weigh very much."

I smiled, impressed. "Not at all. I was thinking the same thing. We have someone who was both slight and angry."

Fleur opened her eyes, and I nodded to the shape, which had now taken on the outline of a human. "It looks female," she said, and I shook my head.

"Benjamin is also very slight, so I don't think we can discount him as a suspect yet."

"Do you really think this is the aura of the person who killed Tanya?" Fleur asked as she gaped at the misplaced energy.

"I can't know that for sure. But given the anger, we both feel coming from it, and that the bricks couldn't have made it over the roof without a helping hand, I do believe this is someone who wanted to hurt Aaron. We'd better get back to the house and call him."

I dropped my hands from Fleur's, pocketed the stones, and took a deep breath. Without our minds focused on it, the trace of the aura faded. I was about to climb back over the edge of the roof and onto the scaffolding when Fleur placed a hand on my shoulder. She opened and closed her mouth as though wanting to say something, but her gaze fell to her feet.

"What is it?" I asked.

"I think we're both assuming that whoever tried to hurt

Aaron was also the person who killed Tanya."

"I guess we are, even though we have no proof. And?"

"It's just, you met him for the first time yesterday, correct?" I nodded, and she continued. "And he's gorgeous and charming, but you saw what his mum's like. Maybe he isn't as nice as we think he is. I mean, you're gorgeous too, but you've got awfully close to him in such a short space of time."

I bristled, but had to agree. "What are you saying?" I asked.

"I'm saying that maybe Aaron killed Tanya and is staying close to you to influence your investigation. Maybe whoever pushed the bricks and tried to hurt Aaron knows what he did and hates him for it."

I bit my lip and pondered her words. "That's a big conclusion to jump to. Do you—"

"I'm not jumping to any conclusions. I just don't think we should rule out the possibility that Aaron isn't all he appears to be. We can't jump to any conclusions at the moment, can we? And discounting him as a suspect is doing just that. After all, they did date."

I took a deep breath and looked out over the dark, night-time. The sky was a tranquil black, dotted with the occasional star. Glare from the streetlights warmed the village with their orange glow. I tilted my head skywards. My mind whirled with the possibility of her words. Fleur was right. We couldn't jump to conclusions. Not to guilt and not to innocence.

CHAPTER NINE

Fleur's words echoed in my mind as I opened the door to my cottage. Niles greeted me with a tail twitch and circled my ankles. I smiled and picked him up.

"I wish you'd met Aaron for more than the few minutes he was in the store. Maybe then you'd be able to give me some insight into his character," I said while he nuzzled under my chin. "It's just the two of us tonight." Fleur had taken Abby to the flat to keep her company for the night at my suggestion. "I'm peckish. How about a nice bit of chicken as a treat and we curl up and watch some TV together?"

Niles mewed in response, and I deposited him on the

kitchen counter. He watched me intently as I pulled some roast chicken from the fridge and placed a few pieces on a saucer before handing it to him. I made myself a sandwich with the rest and took my plate into the lounge. After flicking on the TV and surfing over twenty channels in three minutes, I muted the sound and stared at the screen while eating my sandwich.

"The thing is," I said to Niles when he jumped on my lap and kneaded it for a few seconds before curling into a ball. "Fleur's right. I really don't know Aaron at all. Plus, he was quick to ingratiate himself into my life as soon as I mentioned that Tanya was murdered."

Niles stretched out a paw and placed it on my belly, his way of providing some comfort and showing he was listening while at the same time closing his eyes and appearing asleep. His soft, soothing purr vibrated against my legs and washed all the stress from my body. I'd read somewhere that a cat's purr has healing properties, and I didn't for a moment doubt it wasn't true.

"Someone threw those bricks at him," I said. "I'll never get Kate to believe me. I think you'd like her. She can come across as a little cold and standoffish, but I think that's just how she has to act given her job. I just wish there was a way I could persuade her Aaron's in danger. Someone has already tried to kill him once. It's only a matter of time before they try again."

I stroked Niles on the head and tickled behind his ear,

causing it to twitch, while pondering the possibility of creating a spell to make her believe me. I shook the thought from my head and berated myself. First, I'd considered messing with Fleur's mind to make her forget she'd seen Niles shift, and now this. It was unconscionable to use magic to manipulate people. Doing so would make me no better than my ex with his con games.

I huffed out a deep breath and saw a flash of Idris Elba step out from behind an ambulance on the TV. He pulled a phone from his pocket and pressed it to his ear.

"You're right, Luther," I said, referring to his character on the screen. "The best thing to do is call Aaron and tell him what Fleur and I found." After all, I'd already taken one move out of Luther's playbook and broken into a property. I might as well take his actions as guidance to get on the phone.

After dropping my head back in the chair, I closed my eyes before taking a couple of deep breaths. I'd have to move Niles to get the phone, but he likely knew that having heard me talking to the TV and would move of his own accord in a few minutes. I was in no rush. After what happened with his mother, Aaron might not be willing to take my call, anyway.

Those restful few minutes were shortened by the doorbell ringing.

Niles stepped onto the arm of the chair and started preening himself while I went to see who was calling. A knot formed in my stomach as I entered the hall. This would be my first visitor to the house if you discounted Fleur, and she hadn't rung the bell. I really hoped it wouldn't turn out to be the police or someone equally ominous.

I opened the door and was pleased to see Aaron beaming at me. "I know it's late," he said. "But I wanted to check in and see how you were."

I pushed the door wide for him and invited him in. "Would you care for a drink?" I asked and headed straight for the drinks cabinet to fix myself a gin and tonic.

"I'd love a whiskey if you have any," he said.

"I do." I poured both our drinks and stared at myself in the mirror that backed the top two shelves. Sheesh, I looked tired, and I won't even go into the feral nature of my hair. I took a deep breath and shifted my gaze to the two drinks. "Have you... um... spoken to your mother this evening?" I asked, unsure if I wanted the answer.

Aaron cleared his throat and confirmed that he had. "She's not your biggest fan at the moment," he said, and I laughed. That might be an understatement.

"She said she was going to tell you to stay away from me."

"She did."

"But you came anyway." I couldn't help the small swell of elation that warmed my body and rejuvenated my tired mind, no more than I could help the rush of paranoia that followed it. Aaron had stopped seeing Tanya on the say-so of his mum. Why would I be any different? Unless he needed to stay close to me to stop me from finding her killer.

My gaze shifted to a flash of movement in the mirror and I saw Aaron sit in my armchair with Niles still perched on the arm. He gently stroked between Niles's ears with the back of his hand. In return, my cat leaned his head back and nudged the hand with his nose. I smiled. Niles liked him.

"Did she tell you what happened?" I asked as I handed him the glass of whiskey.

"She's having a hard time accepting Tanya might have been murdered, that's all," he answered.

I sat on the sofa to the side of the TV and nodded before taking a sip from my glass. I wanted to bring up how disgracefully she'd treated Fleur, but telling someone their mum was racist probably wasn't the best way to convince them they're in danger.

"I'm sorry if she treated your apprentice badly," he said, as if reading my mind. "She has some old-fashioned ideas about many things."

"Racism isn't an idea, it's discrimination and prejudice."

Aaron shifted uncomfortably in the chair and downed his whiskey, making me feel a tad guilty. It wasn't Aaron I should be having a go at; it was his mother. Niles jumped to the floor. He turned my way and gave me a pointed look before padding to the snug off the room. He glanced at me again and blinked slowly before pawing the door open and entering. My brow furrowed. I'd made the snug into a workshop of sorts and used it to mix my spells. Niles heading there now had to mean something.

"Any chance of another one of these?" Aaron asked, breaking my chain of thought.

"Of course." I smiled and shifted to move, but Aaron jumped to his feet and stopped me.

"I can get it. You enjoy your drink," he said before offering me a top-up as well.

I took him up on the offer and decided now would be as good a time as any to fill him in on what Fleur and I discovered, leaving out the bit about magic and instead focusing on how the bricks were too far from the edge to have fallen.

Aaron listened intently and asked for another drink as soon as I'd finished talking. He poured one and instantly downed it before pouring himself another.

"What made you think to check out the roof?" he asked, his voice cold.

"I kept thinking about what happened and became convinced I'd seen a flash of movement from above before the bricks fell," I said. "And then Fleur and I spoke to the workmen and when they mentioned not being able to go inside until an inspection confirmed it was safe—"

"If it wasn't safe for them, it wasn't safe for you. Anything could have happened." Aaron shook his head and retook his seat.

"It was fine. They were just concerned about Health & Safety regulations. We weren't in any danger." I placed my empty glass on the side table and sat forward. "None of that matters. The only thing that does is that someone tried to kill you. I have to believe that's connected to Tanya's death." The idea that two unrelated killers were roaming the sleepy village was too ridiculous to fathom.

Aaron rubbed a hand over his head. He looked as tired as I felt. I glanced at the clock on the mantle, noted it was twenty past ten, and stifled a yawn. My bedtime was long gone.

"I'm not sure what to think or say. None of what you say makes sense." Aaron cleared his throat and stared at me. "Don't get angry," he said, three words that guaranteed whatever he said next would make me angry. "Is there a possibility this is all in your head?"

"What?"

He sat forward, leaning across the gap between us to take my hand. "Given your history with your ex, is there a chance that you're seeing crimes where none are being committed?"

"No. That's not what's happening. Tanya was murdered."

"How do you know Tanya was murdered? The police thought it was an accident. And now the bricks. The building is derelict. That scaffolding has been up for almost two years that I can remember. I know your ex hurt you, but you have to trust that people are good again. You can't live your life convinced every accident is an attempt at murder."

I pulled my hands away, not sure how to respond. I opened and closed my mouth, waiting for words to come out. Aaron looked like he was about to say something, but Niles darted into the living room, yowling, and barrelled into the door leading to the hall, practically knocking it from its hinges. The smell of smoke and fire that hit us as soon as he did had both me and Aaron jumping from our seats and rushing to see what was happening.

My heart raced. Flames licked the front door, spreading up from the letterbox and engulfing the surrounding wood. The carpet flared in one spot and the unmistakable stench of paraffin filled the air. I coughed in the smoke and froze, unsure what to do. If it weren't for Aaron standing beside me, I wouldn't hesitate to use my magic.

"There's a fire extinguisher in the kitchen," I said. To punctuate my words, the fire alarm finally did its job and detected the smoke, adding a blaring alarm to muddle my thoughts.

Niles jumped into my arms. And, without a word, Aaron turned and ran to the kitchen. The paint bubbled and oozed a black smoke, and the flames reached out beyond the door, caressing the frame as if hungry to devour all that it could. Not wanting to wait and see my new home further destroyed, I lifted my hand and used my magic to suffocate the flames. They dwindled to nothing.

It was only then that I realised Aaron was taking a long time to retrieve the fire extinguisher. Holding tight to Niles, I ran to find out what was holding him up and found him battling a second blaze at the back door.

"Eira," Fleur called from outside. "Can you hear me? I've called the fire brigade. They should be here soon. Are you okay? Can you get out a window?"

"We're okay," I shouted.

With Aaron's back to me, I gave him a helping hand in dousing this fire with my magic. The second the last ember faded to nothing, he turned and ran from the kitchen, ready to tackle the blaze at the front door, but returned moments later when he discovered it no longer burning.

I coughed again. The fire may be out, but the acrid smoke remained. Aaron kicked through the charred wood of the back door and we made our way outside into the fresh air.

Fleur ran up and hugged me. Niles wriggled between us and

jumped to the floor.

"What on Earth happened?" she asked.

I glanced at Aaron, who eyed me wearily. "Do you still think it's all in my mind?" I said.

He huffed out a breath and shook his head. "One fire might be an accident, but two and covering both the exits, not a chance."

A siren blared in the distance. Moments later, a fire engine pulled up at the front of the house.

Twenty minutes later, Kate McIntyre arrived. She spoke to the firemen before coming over to us.

"It looks like arson," she said. "The crew commander suspects paraffin was used as an accelerant. The front and back doors both look to have been doused with more poured through the letterbox. Do you want to tell me what's going on?"

Fleur looked at her feet, and Aaron looked at me. I sighed and noted again my belief that someone had tried to kill Aaron. Kate's eyes never left my own, but her forehead furrowed and the scowl on her face grew as I spoke.

"I'll overlook the trespass and breaking and entering, for now," she said before placing her hands on her hips and huffing air out of her nostrils. She glanced at my cottage. "I'd say whoever did this was after more than just Mr Jenkins here," she said. "I told you not to meddle," she added as she pulled a phone from her pocket and moved away from us a few steps.

Even so, I couldn't help but hear her ask for Benjamin. It was clear from her follow up question that he wasn't there. I darted my gaze to Aaron but refrained from asking the question burning through my mind. The same question must have occurred to him as he shook his head and mumbled, "Ben wouldn't have done this."

"Have you seen him at all today?" Kate asked, returning.

"He came by the store this morning," I answered.

"What time was that?"

"Around nine-thirty. He left with—"

Aaron raised his hand as though in a school class. "Me," he said. "I took him to my mother's. We arranged to speak to a solicitor. He was worried about his interview with you. Trisha called shortly after with figures for the funeral. That stressed him out even further."

"I imagine it would," I said. Funerals were not cheap, and from what Susan said about the state of Tanya's finances, Benjamin would struggle to pay.

"After that," Aaron continued, "I dropped him at his place in Cardiff to get cleaned up. When I went back for him this afternoon, he'd already left."

"What time was that?" Kate asked.

"The appointment with the solicitor was set for half past

one, so it must have been around ten to. I wondered if he'd seen the solicitor without me, but they called. He was a no show."

"He didn't show for our scheduled four o'clock interview either," Kate added.

Aaron was adamant that Benjamin couldn't be involved in setting the fires, but the look on his face belied his doubts. Fleur mentioned his outburst in the shop this morning, and Kate's ears pricked at the news. The conversation dwindled after that. The crew commander said the fire crew would be leaving. They'd collected samples from the doors and would confirm tomorrow if paraffin was definitely used.

Kate excused herself, too, after confirming where Aaron and I would be staying, and arranging for a police car to drive by every hour. Eventually, only Fleur and I stood in the garden.

"Are you sure you don't want to spend the night in the flat?" she asked. "I can sleep on the sofa."

I glanced at my cottage and shook my head. "I'll be fine in my own bed. Niles will keep me company and warn me if there's any danger."

"Okay. If you're sure. Goodnight."

"Goodnight, Fleur."

Niles trailed me back to the cottage. The smell of burning lingered in the air. But luckily, with neither a front nor back door, the fresh air would wash out the smell in no time. I'd just need an extra blanket on the bed to stop myself from freezing.

CHAPTER TEN

Niles woke me the next morning by jumping on my back and kneading my hair. I opened my eyes, saw the light seeping around the curtains, and turned to the bedside clock. Realising it was past ten, I groaned. I should have opened the shop over an hour ago. I debated closing my eyes and going back to sleep, but Niles' clawing intensified, and he caught my scalp a time or two. Knowing he wouldn't wait much longer for food, I rolled, making him jump to the side, and climbed out of bed.

With my slippers firmly on my feet and my dressing gown wrapped as tight as it could go, I headed downstairs. Before we made it to the kitchen, Niles darted ahead and pawed at the door to the snug. It was then I remembered his trip to the room last night, and I knew he wanted to tell me something.

"What is it, boy?" I asked and pushed inside.

Apothecary cabinets lined the walls, filled with jars containing too many different concoctions to note. Niles jumped on the worktable in the middle of the room and hopped to one of the cabinets. He walked along the shelf looking at all the jars before stopping and purring smugly at one. Within the blink of an eye, he'd reached out a paw and swatted it from the shelf.

I sighed and flicked my hand at the jar to stop it from smashing on the floor. It floated towards me and I reached out to catch it. "Copaiba." I read the label and furrowed my brow. Copaiba was great for soothing anxious feelings and supporting the nervous system. Unlike many essential oils, it wasn't dangerous to cats, which is why I'd used it to make the soothing potion Mrs Jenkins had asked me to deliver for her neighbour's cat. "What is it you want me to know?" I asked and absent-mindedly unscrewed the top and took a whiff.

My stomach churned as its sweet, woody scent hit me. Aaron... Aaron smelt like the oil. That's why his scent had been so familiar to me. But what did that mean? Was he wearing it? He never mentioned having a cat himself, and Mrs Jenkins said the oil was for a neighbour. My mind churned, trying to make sense of the thoughts flooding through it.

"He was wearing the soothing balm I gave to Mrs Jenkins last night. That's what you wanted to tell me."

Niles gave me a superior, pointed look and jumped down from the cabinet. I placed the bottle back on the shelf and followed him to the kitchen.

Why would Aaron be wearing the oil? Tanya said that Abby didn't like many people. Aaron had said something similar himself. He could be wearing it to make her calm around him. But I'd noticed the scent on him at our first meeting. How could he have known Abby would be at the shop with me? I shook my head. I was jumping to conclusions. There could be any number of reasons why he was wearing the oil.

My heart almost leapt into my throat when the phone rang, interrupting my thoughts.

"Hello," I answered, and instantly felt guilty for how sharp my voice sounded.

"Ms Snow, it's Detective Inspector Kate McIntyre. I wanted to call and make sure everything was okay. Plus, if you haven't found someone to replace your doors already, I have the number for a reliable contractor you can call."

"Oh, that would be fabulous. Thank you, Inspector. Truth be told, I'm only just out of bed, so I haven't done anything yet." I wrote down the details of the contractor Kate recommended and said I would call them immediately. "Thank you," I said again and was about to say goodbye when Kate mentioned locating Benjamin.

I perched on a stool when my legs became shaky at the sound of her voice. "Is everything all right?" I asked, twiddling my pen in my hand.

"He's fine. He was arrested for being drunk and disorderly in Cardiff yesterday afternoon. Spent the afternoon and most of the night in a cell."

"Oh, that's... well... as long as he's okay."

"He's fine. It also means he's not your arsonist." It was only then I understood her tone. Kate had banked on Benjamin being the guilty party, and I had to admit, with his attitude and tempestuous nature, so had I. "A police car will drive by and keep watch on your place throughout the day, and I'll try to get someone stationed outside tonight. In the meantime, keep me posted if you go anywhere and stay somewhere public if you can. If you can get the contractors in today, that would add some extra bodies at your place to deter anyone from trying anything."

While she talked, only one thought circled through my mind. If Benjamin wasn't the killer, was Aaron? I debated telling Kate about the cat oil, but shook the thought from my mind. Aaron had been with me. Even if he was Tanya's killer, and I couldn't wrap my head around that concept, he couldn't be the arsonist, and he couldn't have pushed the bricks at himself.

Instead of saying anything, I thanked Kate again, ended the call and immediately arranged for the contractors to come over. After a quick breakfast, I showered and dressed and used the remaining twenty minutes I had before they arrived to check in on Fleur and the store. I had already resigned myself to the fact we wouldn't be opening the store, but was pleasantly surprised to find that Fleur had opened on time and had even processed the online orders for the day.

I told her about Benjamin and asked if she fancied a walk later. "We might also indulge in a little info gathering while we're at it," I said. I couldn't ask Aaron for help. Not with the way I was doubting him, at the moment.

Fleur agreed. We closed the store and headed back to the cottage to wait for the contractors. As soon as they arrived, they set to work. I sent a quick text to Kate to let her know I'd be around the village for a short while, and we headed out.

"Where are we going?" Fleur asked as soon as we turned onto the high street and walked past the front of the shop.

"We're visiting Susan Reynolds. She lives down the road in Ponthir. It shouldn't take more than thirty to forty minutes to walk there." At least that's how long it had taken me to reach it when I delivered her a balm the other night.

Fleur nodded and pointed at the Roman Baths across the road. "Have you had time to visit the baths yet?" she asked, and I shook my head. "When this is all over, we should go."

"Have you been?" I asked.

"Not yet. I only came through the village in passing less than a week ago when I saw Crystal Magic." She laughed and shrugged. "I couldn't have imagined then that I'd soon be living here."

"You're from Bristol originally, aren't you?"

Fleur gave me a wonky smile, and in her thick Bristolian accent said, "Brizzle born an' proud, me babber." I laughed, guessing more than actually knowing what she said. "My mate has a flat in Cwmbran. I was on my way there."

"And your parents — are they still in Bristol?"

"Nah, they're long gone."

"I am sor—"

"They're not dead," she added quickly. "Just gone, and good riddance."

"I'm from here originally," I said. "I guess I've probably been to the baths. I just don't remember."

"Then we'll definitely have to visit. I wish I knew more about the area. I'd never even heard of the place before I came through."

"We'll have to remedy that."

The air felt invigorating and fresh as we walked around the

common, with its beautifully trimmed grass and a spattering of trees. I told Fleur what little I knew of the village.

Caerleon was once home to the Roman fortress of Isca, which dated all the way back to 74 AD when the first timber encampment was erected to subdue the tribes living in Wales. The baths were the remains of that fortress, as was the amphitheatre found off one of the side roads. The prolonged war with the Silures, the local iron-age tribe, had proved costly to the Romans. Caerleon was steeped in history, and parts of the fortress wall still stood, with the stone from other parts having been repurposed hundreds of years ago to make some of the buildings we passed.

"Some also link the village to King Arthur," I added, remembering how my mother had been full of tales of Merlin, Morgana, and the legendary king. I'd always soaked in her every word. Maybe the witch in me enjoyed hearing tales of other magic folks. Fleur's ears certainly pricked at the mention.

The walk to Susan's seemed far quicker with company than when I'd journeyed it alone and we soon arrived. Susan answered, looking far more put together than the last times I saw her.

"Eira." She flung the door wide and pulled me in for a hug.

"I just thought I'd call in and see how you were doing," I said before introducing Fleur.

To my relief, Susan smiled warmly at her and pulled her in for a hug of greeting, too. She ushered us both into the living room and offered us a drink. Fleur perched nervously on the chenille sofa, which was the soft pink, semi violet hue of the Kunzite crystal. She looked around the plush room as though her presence could make everything valuable spontaneously shatter. It was becoming more and more clear to me that Fleur wasn't someone used to having nice surroundings.

"You're looking a lot better," I said as Susan handed me a cup of peppermint tea.

Susan's smile faltered a little, but she plastered it straight back on. "It comes and goes in waves," she said. "I'm not sure how I would have coped without that balm you gave me. It's almost magical."

Fleur's eyes darted to mine, and I took a sip of my tea. "Not at all," I said, and winked at Fleur. "I actually have an ulterior motive for coming rather than just seeing how you are," I added. "Fleur's my apprentice. She'll soon be busy learning how to make balms like the one I gave you, and also lives in the flat above my shop. I wanted the two of you to meet as Abby has taken rather a shine to Fleur, and I suspect she has taken to Abby as well. I really think they'd be well suited to each other and wanted to make sure it was okay with you if Abby lives with Fleur. She won't find a more loving home."

Fleur did that strange thing where she looked worried and yet excited at the same time.

Susan smiled at her. "From the look on your face," she said. "I wouldn't dream of doing anything but approve. Tanya would be pleased that Abby has found someone who cares for her as much as she did. And if Abby likes you, who am I to argue with her choice?" Susan sat on the sofa next to Fleur and took her hand. "You must be a little magical yourself for that cat to like you."

Fleur beamed at her, and I hid my smile by taking another sip of tea. "Aaron mentioned Abby being difficult around people as well," I said, "but I have to confess, she's been an absolute sweetie around us."

"Maybe her disappearance soothed her temper somewhat. Although, then again..." she sighed and flung herself back dramatically in the seat. "Maybe she was disagreeable because of Tanya. Tanya very much hated having anyone in her house. She was extremely private and never liked to bring her male friends home. Having a cat that behaved aggressively to everyone it met was a convenient excuse to keep people out."

"Her sister mentioned she was dating," I said and faltered, not sure how to delicately bring up that she was dating more than one man.

Susan smiled at me knowingly. "It's okay," she said. "I've known Tanya for a very long time. We went to school together.

There was a short period when I went to college that we drifted apart, but we soon became close again after my return. I know everything she did and who she did it with."

"Did you know Frank and David well?" I asked, and wondered if Trisha had managed to reach David yet.

"I know Frank. He's been on the scene for years. David, well, David, I've only met a few times. He doesn't come around very often, but when he does, they spend all their time together. Tanya was always very secretive about their relationship, even from me. But I never got the impression she expected him to stick around."

"Why?" Fleur asked, sitting back in the seat next to Susan, and looking relaxed for the first time.

"David likes to spend money. Tanya liked to have money spent on her. They went on meals together, a few day trips, and then he'd be gone until the next visit, whenever that may be." Fleur nodded and asked if it was the same with Frank. I pondered whether David could have a poor wife somewhere. His behaviour with Tanya sounded very much like the way Chris would treat his mistresses. "No. Tanya actually had genuine feelings for Frank. Not in the way you think," Susan added when I opened my mouth to say something. "He was sweet, lonely. He lost his wife and needed some company in his life. Tanya hated to see such a good man sad."

"Trisha mentioned that he might have wanted to marry Tanya," I said and looked for somewhere to place my empty cup.

Noting my search, Susan took it from my hand and placed it on the glass table next to the sofa. "There was never a chance of Frank and Tanya marrying. Neither of them wanted that." She scoffed. "No, in his mind, Frank is still married to his wife. He could never replace her."

"Then neither were serious relationships," I said, feeling a little deflated.

From what she said, I couldn't see either Frank or David having a reason to kill Tanya. Maybe David's wife, if he had one. But if she was anything like me, she would have reserved that special kind of hate for the husband who betrayed her. I was beginning to think my original assertion was correct, after all. Maybe it was just a random killing. Someone could have found Abby and demanded the £10,000 reward. With Tanya unable to pay, a fatal argument ensued. It might explain why Tanya hadn't mentioned who killed her. The truth was, she didn't know.

Susan leaned her head back and sighed, and I felt a little guilty dragging her through all the questions. "Tanya hasn't had a serious relationship since Julie," she said.

"Julie!" Fleur and I said at the same time.

"I suppose there's no point in keeping her secret anymore. Tanya and Julie met when I was in college. They were very much in love and practically inseparable. If Julie hadn't died... Anyway," Susan sat forward and gave me a wry smile, "Julie Mosley was Tanya's one and only serious relationship. She was the only person she ever truly loved."

"Including her husband?" Fleur asked.

"Phillip was someone she settled on to keep Trisha happy. After Julie died, she didn't have the energy to fight her anymore." With that, she stood, walked over to the cabinet, and pulled out a bottle of vodka. "Would you care for a drink? I know it's early, but as they say, 'it's six o'clock somewhere'."

Feeling guilty for driving her to drink, I accepted and resolved to stay for a while to make sure she didn't overindulge. Fleur accepted too, and we found ourselves sipping vodka and tonic at lunchtime.

"I'm famished," Susan announced after our fourth drink. "Let's order in. The Goldcroft does a fabulous bacon and Brie ciabatta."

She sashayed to the kitchen to fetch a menu, while I mulled over everything she'd said. It was then I remembered her saying she felt the way Tanya felt when Julie passed, and I suddenly realised that Susan loved Tanya. They'd drifted apart when she was in college, but that was the same time Julie came into the picture. I almost cursed myself for thinking it, but I suddenly wondered if Susan could have killed her. I'd been ready to believe

Frank was a lover scorned. Why not Susan?

I plastered a smile on my face for her return and we ordered food. Susan was so nice; I couldn't believe her a killer. But how hard must it be to spend decades by the side of someone you loved and know they would never reciprocate your feelings? I think it would eat the best of us up inside.

Susan poured us all another drink and alcohol-infused paranoia kicked in. I looked at my glass, skewed-eyed, and imagined her poisoning us. It was only when she wiped a tear from her eye that rational thought returned. Aaron might have been wrong when he accused the murder of being all in my head, but he might also have been right when he said my relationship with my ex was clouding my judgement. Good people were sometimes just that, good people. Not everyone was hiding their true nature.

"I can't believe she's gone," Susan said. "In the blink of an eye, everything changes. You'd think I'd have learnt that after Julie died in the fire."

"Fire?" Fleur sat forward, clutching her spell infused pendulum. "The fire was deliberate, wasn't it?" she said.

My hand flew to my mouth.

"How could you know that?" Susan asked, blinking in confusion.

"I-I don't know, just a hunch."

"Well, it's a *bleeping* good one. Julie died when her flat caught fire. The police said an accelerant was used."

"Paraffin?" I asked.

"I wouldn't know the details. Just that no one was ever caught." Susan looked between Fleur and me and rubbed at her forehead. "What are you thinking?" she asked. "Julie's death was two decades ago. You can't possibly think Tanya's death is in any way connected to that."

The doorbell rang, announcing the arrival of our food, and Susan went to answer, while directing Fleur and me to the kitchen to gather some plates.

"Cupboard above the breadboard," she shouted through the house.

"Do you think Julie's death is related to Tanya's?" Fleur asked. I looked at her pendulum. "Do you?" I countered. To which Fleur nodded. "Then I trust your intuition. We just need to figure out how two murders two decades apart can possibly be connected."

When Susan returned, I decided to share my belief that Tanya was murdered. Thankfully, she already knew, as the Detective Inspector had been in touch. She was convinced I was right, declaring Tanya too experienced in walking in heels to fall down the stairs. However, she was sceptical of any connection between Julie's death and Tanya's, but eventually conceded that both of them being murdered might be more than a coincidence.

"It was so long ago. Too many of the details have been forgotten. I was in London, studying at the time, and only heard bits and bobs. Tanya never liked to talk about it. Julie's death caused her too much pain." Susan sighed and took a bite of her bacon and Brie ciabatta.

I'd opted for smashed avocado and grilled halloumi on mine and had to say, it was delicious.

Fleur had gone all out with bacon, egg, and sausage. "Old newspaper stories might help with some of the details," she said between mouthfuls.

"Will we be able to access them?"

She shrugged. "Some will be online. It depends on how far we need to go back."

"Autumn term, 1995," Susan interjected. "I can't remember the exact month, but I remember it was before Christmas, and it was the year before Tanya married Phillip. I think I have a picture of us all together."

Susan disappeared into the living room for a few minutes and came back with a photo album. She placed it on the kitchen table and flicked through the pages until she found what she wanted. "Here we are?" she said and flashed a sad smile before pushing the picture across the table to us. "It was taken the day after I arrived home for the summer break. The first time I met

Julie in person. We were in a nightclub in Newport. Ritzys, I think."

Four young women stared out from the photo, smiling. The club behind them was dark but full of people with the glare of lights over their heads. I recognised Julie instantly. She was the mirror image of her ghost form. I guessed which ones were Tanya and Susan, as they still held a familiar semblance about them, but the fourth woman in the black bra top and hot-pants was a mystery. "Who's this?" I asked Susan.

"That's Trisha, Tanya's sister."

As she said the words, I noted her familial resemblance to Tanya, but it was hard to equate the image of the young lady before me with the buttoned-up woman she'd become. "I'd never have recognised her," I said.

Susan gave a wry chuckle. "She has changed. You can thank her husband for that. Tim's quite the prude on the quiet, with some old-fashioned ideas regarding the way women should dress and behave." She took a sip of her vodka, which was now devoid of tonic, and continued, "Trisha went to the university. It was her that made friends with Julie first and introduced her to Tanya. She lasted until the Christmas after Julie's death. She'd met Tim the Easter before, if I remember correctly, and he didn't see a point in her continuing her studies. They have no children, but he insisted she never worked outside the house. He believes the wife's role is in the home. They'd be a good deal better off if Trisha did work, especially with the financial trouble Tim's business is in." Susan sighed and shook her head. "We used to be close, but not anymore. In those days, she had the same zest for life as Tanya. She always had an obsessive streak to her personality, and as soon as she met Tim, she dedicated her whole life to him."

She smiled wistfully and put the photograph back in her album. "What will you do if the online newspaper records don't go back far enough?" she asked, to move the conversation in a different direction.

"We might need to look at microfiche versions going back that far. The library should hold them."

Susan nodded. "You'll need to go to the central library in Newport."

We all sobered following our food, and Susan announced the need for some sleep, so Fleur and I excused ourselves and walked home.

CHAPTER ELEVEN

Fleur was feeling pumped and eager to continue our investigation. I was feeling exhausted. Drinking in the afternoon was never a good idea. Not all of us had the alcohol tolerance and energy of a nineteen-year-old. After she checked her phone and said that the library opened late on Saturdays, so she still had a good few hours before it closed, I gave her £50 and told her to get a taxi to Newport. Anything she could find out about Julie might prove useful.

She darted off while I headed to the cottage. The contractors were still there. They'd finished the back door and were now working at the front. The sound as they hammered and drilled pierced my brain and drove me to the medicine cabinet. Much like Susan, I could have done with an afternoon nap to recuperate, but there was no chance of that, so I settled for some magically infused ginseng tea.

I grabbed my phone and the tea and headed into the garden to gain some fresh air and escape the noise.

"Detective Inspector," I said as soon as Kate answered. "I'm calling to let you know I'm back home and to thank you again for the workers you recommended. They have done a terrific job so far." I sat on the edge of the patio step and sipped my tea. Niles and Abby both joined me.

"I've managed to get a detail to watch over the house tonight," Kate said.

"That's great news. Any luck in finding the person responsible?"

"Inquiries are ongoing," Kate said, her voice strained.

"That's a no then."

"Any luck your end?" she asked.

I stretched out my legs and took a deep swig of tea. "I'm not sure what you're asking?" I said and smirked.

"Hmm, hmm. There's not one doubt in my mind that you've been out and about meddling in my case again," she said. "So, I'm a little curious about what you discovered."

"Well, for one, I discovered that Tanya was a lesbian or

bisexual. I'm not entirely sure which."

"And this is relevant because...?"

"Because it was a secret. I might not be Miss Marple or some great Detective Inspector, but even I know that secrets often lead to trouble, and you can't get more trouble than murder." I finished my tea and placed the empty cup on the ground beside me. My head swirled, and I braced myself to stop from falling over. "I also discovered that the love of her life was killed in a deliberate fire over twenty years ago. The police never caught the arsonist responsible."

Kate laughed before apologising. "And you've decided my case is connected to this old one. How?" she asked.

"I have no idea, but I bet if we find out, we'll find a killer."

Kate huffed down the line, and I could practically feel the battle raging inside her head. One side eventually won, and she asked for details of the old murder. I gave her all we had, which amounted to a name and rough date, and she vowed to investigate it.

I ended the call, lay down on the cold stone of the patio, and stared at the sky. It was remarkably blue with only the odd wispy cloud to mar its splendour. I closed my eyes and took a few deep breaths, wondering if I could stay where I was and sleep for the rest of the day, when someone cleared their throat.

I opened my eyes and strained my head back to see an

upside-down Aaron framed in my back door. He wore a nice green polo shirt with the neck undone and a pair of blue jeans. His hair flopped onto his forehead and formed a little kiss-curl. "Do you mind if I join you?" he asked.

I scrunched my eyes and looked at him curiously. "Do you mind if I ask you a question?" I countered.

"Oh, sounds ominous." He approached with a curious look on his face and sat on the patio step next to me.

I sat up and sniffed. His face became... curiouser... Is that a word? Hmm? Curiouser and curiouser. If it's good enough for Lewis Carroll, it's good enough for me. His face became curiouser, and I realised I wasn't as sober as I'd believed. "You smell sweet and woody. Did you know that? I love your smell. The only problem is, it's not your smell, is it?"

Aaron smirked at me. "Have you been drinking?" he asked.

"Maybe." I waved my pointed finger in his face. "Stop avoiding the question."

His smirk grew wider, and I resisted the urge to twirl his kiss-curl around my finger. "I'm not entirely sure what your question is," he said.

"My question is why do you smell like the copaiba oil I delivered to your mum for her neighbour's cat? Furthermore, if that cat is Abby, and I suspect it is, why did she want the oil in the first place when Abby was missing?"

Aaron clasped onto my finger, which now pointed directly into his face in accusation, and lowered it. He looked at me seriously. "I don't know what you're talking about," he said. "Mum gave me the oil to help with stress. I've been overworked for a while, which was one of the reasons I was happy to book the week off when she asked."

"Your Mum," my finger rose again, but Aaron pushed it back down, "ordered the oil for her neighbour's stressed-out cat. She did not order it for you." Not that there was any reason it wouldn't work for a human.

Aaron stood and pulled his mobile from his jeans pocket. "Mum!" he said, after a moment. "I'm at Eira's." He pursed his lips and rubbed at his forehead.

I lay back down and closed my eyes, guessing that was the last thing she wanted to hear.

"I don't care about any of that right now," he said. "Was the oil you gave me intended for Abby?"

I couldn't hear Mrs Jenkins' response, but from the tension emanating from Aaron, it couldn't have been pleasant. After a few minutes, he must have ended the call as he came over and tapped me on the leg.

"It was for the cat," I said and opened my eyes.

"It was," he answered, but he didn't look at all pleased with the revelation. "I've got to pop and see Mum. Get some rest. I'll call you later."

I nodded and closed my eyes again. I'm not sure how long I lay there before another person cleared their throat in the doorway. Opening my eyes, half expecting to see that Aaron had returned, I instead discovered that the contractor had finished with my doors and was looking for payment before he could leave.

CHAPTER TWELVE

The next morning had to be the first day in a long time that I had woken feeling refreshed and ready for the day. I had managed more than a full night's sleep! Wow! I think I could count on one hand the times that had happened in the last year. Maybe day drinking was a secret blessing in disguise. Although I resolved it was best not to make a habit of it. Instead of Niles waking me, I snuggled into him and petted him for a good twenty minutes while he decided whether he was ready to head down for breakfast or not.

Even though it was Sunday, I headed to the store to assess what needed to be replaced for the week ahead. Fleur ran down to greet me, but when I told her she didn't have to work, she insisted that she wanted to learn all the ropes. "Tea? Coffee?" I offered, as I flicked the sign to 'open'. If we were both going to be in the store, we might as well be available should any customers wander by.

"I'm fine, thanks. I just grabbed a cuppa upstairs." Fleur bobbed on her tiptoes and called to Abby to see if she was coming. Abby padded down the stairs and jumped on the sofa. Fleur sat next to her and asked what our plans were concerning Tanya's murder.

"I haven't really thought that far ahead," I admitted and sat in the armchair opposite her. I'd have to find out what happened between Aaron and his mum. That's if he was willing to talk to me. I wasn't one-hundred percent sober when we talked yesterday and although I pretty much remembered what happened, things were a little fuzzy around the edges. One thing I did know is that he was not terribly pleased when he left, and despite his promised call, one never materialised. "Ooh, did you find out anything about Julie?" I asked, remembering Fleur's trip to the library yesterday.

"I'd be curious to know what you found too," Kate said, having appeared from nowhere. She closed the shop door and took the seat next to mine.

I glanced at the top of the door, confused as to why the

bell hadn't sounded to announce her arrival, but remembered Benjamin had broken it and I hadn't had the chance to fix it yet. I should have asked the contractors to do it when they were replacing my cottage doors.

"Good morning, Kate," I said, deciding that as she had simply walked in and taken a seat, our relationship must have progressed beyond the point where I needed to call her Detective Inspector.

"Morning, Eira," she said, shrugging out of her suit jacket. "And Fleur, isn't it?" Fleur nodded, but looked a little nervous. "What did you find out about Julie?" Kate continued.

"Not a lot. The papers mentioned that she was originally from London and was in Caerleon studying at the university. I didn't even know there was a local university."

"There isn't anymore," Kate said. "The campus closed in 2016. There's talk of a housing development now. It's a shame. We used to have a thriving student community."

Fleur sat back, and Abby jumped on her lap. The cat had a soothing effect on her, and she relaxed into her story. "She was staying in the halls of residence when she died," she continued. "The newspaper mentioned that she was on the third floor and that her door had been doused in paraffin and set alight. Other than that, there were very few details. They mentioned she'd been on a night out with friends and had visited a few clubs in the city. She also had family in London. Parents and a brother. That's it. I scanned through every newspaper covering the eight months after her death. The story was on the front page for a few days. After that, it slipped to page seven and then disappeared altogether."

"I'm impressed," Kate said. "Very thorough. You should consider a career in the force."

"Hey, get your own apprentice," I quipped while smiling at Fleur, who looked sheepishly at her feet. "Seriously, Fleur. It's really impressive that you took the time to search through all those papers."

"If Tanya was killed by the same person who killed Julie, then it couldn't have been Benjamin," I said, stating the obvious, as Niles jumped on the arm of the chair beside me.

"As well as being in a jail cell at the time someone set the fires at your place, he also has an alibi for the time of Tanya's death. The pathology report came back and placed her death as between 12:30 and 2 p.m. Benjamin was giving a presentation in his experimental physics class. His half-an-hour slot was booked starting at ten past twelve. He watched other members of his class give their presentations for the rest of the time. I have two lecturers and seventeen students who will swear he was in the lecture hall from ten in the morning all the way to three in the afternoon."

"Then why was he so worried about being questioned?" I asked.

"I asked him the same thing. He'd assumed his mother had died just before you found her body and didn't have an alibi for the time after he left university."

I pondered her words for a minute and had to admit that I'd assumed the same thing. It was horrible to think of Tanya lying undiscovered for over five hours. My brow furrowed. It was also confusing why no one had seen the door open when I'd easily spotted it. I was about to say as much when Kate continued.

"I also discovered that David Mosley is Julie's brother." She pulled a smug face and steepled her fingers.

I glanced at Fleur, confused. From Kate's demeanour, she'd revealed something significant, but I had no idea what. As Julie's surname was Mosley, I would have assumed her brother's to be as well.

"Wait," said Fleur and clutched her pendulum, which was something else I'd noticed about her. Whenever she had a hunch about something, she would clutch the magically infused pendulum to reassure herself that she might be right. "What's the surname of the David that Tanya was seeing? The one you said her sister had trouble reaching."

I shrugged. I hadn't thought to ask for the surname of either Frank or David.

"That would be David Mosley," Kate answered. "He lives and works in London. He sometimes comes down this way for business. I spoke to his business partner, and he was meant to have been staying at the Celtic Manor for the last nine days, but their records show that he checked out last Wednesday."

Wow! The same day Tanya was killed. I swallowed back a lump in my throat and stroked Niles under the chin. I wasn't sure whether to be glad that we had a definite suspect in sight or disappointed that I hadn't done the work that discovered him. Plus, if he was Tanya's killer and it had to do with his sister's murder, then that's just depressing in a whole other way.

"A warrant's been issued for his arrest. Now we know who we're looking for, we'll find him," Kate said.

Fleur huffed out a breath and clutched tighter to her pendulum.

"What is it?" I asked.

"Nothing." She shook her head and sucked in her bottom lip. "I don't know. I just don't think he did it. Why now? It's been more than twenty years. Susan said he visits every year. But she never mentioned him being Julie's brother. Why not? Plus, there's the whole kidnapped cat angle. Where does that fit in?"

"David Mosley is the only suspect in Tanya's murder without an alibi. Susan, Trisha, Frank and now Benjamin all have people who can vouch for their whereabouts," Kate said. "Sometimes a cat is just a missing cat."

"Yeah, and sometimes an accident is just an accident. Isn't that what you said about the bricks nearly squishing Aaron? Then there's the fire. I've never met or spoken to David, and I don't believe Aaron has either. Why would he try to kill us?"

"I guess we'll have to ask when we bring him in," Kate said, before glancing around and standing. "Is there a ladies' room I could use before heading out?" she added.

"Just through the beaded archway behind the till and to your right," I answered.

"What do we do now?" Fleur asked after Kate disappeared behind the curtains. "Kate clearly thinks she has her man."

"Maybe she does," I said, but rubbed at my temples. My brain wasn't used to all this excess thinking, especially on a Sunday. Sunday's normally a veg-in-front-of-the-TV day. A nagging voice inside my head told me that the only reason David would have to kill Tanya was if he thought she was responsible for Julie's death. Though why he would act after all these years was beyond me. Tanya loved Julie, and vice versa. I'd witnessed that first-hand. There was no way Tanya would have hurt her.

The door slammed open. I turned to the sound and found Mrs Jenkins barrelling in with her nose in the air. I couldn't believe how warm I'd found her the first time we'd met. At the time, she'd been full of allergies, with puffy eyes and a rosy glow to her face. The warm colour had left, and her eyes were no longer soft and friendly but held a mean glare.

I stood, and Fleur rolled her eyes, obviously expecting another confrontation.

"How dare you speak to my son when I told you to stay away from him, and how dare you tell him what I ordered!"

I almost growled in response. "You have no power to tell me what to do," I said, doing a poor job of keeping my anger in check. "And as you were going to tell Aaron to stay away from me, it would seem you have very little power over him too," I added smugly. "As to what you ordered. As your son is wearing it, he has every right to know what it is."

"I'm warning you."

I laughed in incredulous disbelief. She was warning me! From the look on Mrs Jenkins' face, that wasn't something that happened in her presence very often. "You ordered the oil for Abby," I said as soon as I sobered, pointing at the cat whom Fleur now held protectively in her arms. "Why would you order the oil when she'd been missing for days?"

Mrs Jenkins tugged at the necklace around her neck and glanced around as if looking for the answer to my questions. Her eyes fell on Fleur and Abby, and she stiffened. Her lips went thin and her back straightened. "What I do and why is none of your business," she said.

"I'd be curious to know the answer to those questions," Kate said, appearing from between the beaded curtain.

"And I don't see why it would be any of your business either," Mrs Jenkins declared, looking her up and down.

"I don't think you've met Detective Inspector Kate McIntyre, have you?" I stated more than asked. "She's investigating Tanya's death. Her *murder*," I added, emphasising the last word for maximum annoyance. It was petty, but Mrs Jenkins was getting on my last nerve and I'd had enough of her barging into my shop and ordering me around, and don't get me started on the way she looked at Fleur.

Mrs Jenkins fussed with her clothes and looked like she wanted to back out the door. Good. It was about time she squirmed. She was up to something and given the person I'd come to realise she was, it couldn't be anything good. "I-I ordered the oil to help Abby relax. Tanya's sister was afraid to visit her because of that cat. Family should stick by family."

"That would make sense if the cat hadn't been missing for days," I said.

"Well, how was I supposed to know that?" she spluttered.

"I don't know. You'd think someone who put out food for a cat every day would notice her missing." Yeah, that's right, Aaron told me that little tidbit. As I said the words, I realised Aaron had also shared something else with me. I decided to take a wild stab in the dark. "It must have been hard keeping Abby in your house with your cat allergies. You were practically blind with how badly they were swollen on Wednesday."

Mrs Jenkins spluttered something unintelligible. Her eyes flicked to Kate. "I do not have to stand here and take these accusations," she said and turned on her heel and stormed out the door.

"That was interesting," Kate said, and grabbed her jacket from the chair. "I'm not sure you've made a friend there."

"I don't need friends like Samantha Jenkins," I said. Still, a pang of regret welled inside. Any hope of a relationship with Aaron had flown out the window. He cared for his mum a great deal. I could never come between them. "She catnapped Abby," I added.

Kate sighed and shrugged her shoulders. "You might be right. Unfortunately, there's no way to prove it, no owner to make a complaint, and the cat is no longer being held. Locking a cat in your house for a few days doesn't make you a killer," she added when my mouth opened and I was about to protest. "Besides, Mrs Jenkins might be happy to see you dead, but I doubt she'd try to hurt her son."

With that, she left. I plonked down onto the chair and dragged Niles onto my lap. He blinked at me and I petted him under the chin. Kate was right. That didn't mean I had to like it.

"You know what?" I said to Fleur. "It's our day off. We can do this tomorrow. If you don't have other plans and are looking for something to do, we could always make a Sunday lunch at my place, and if you're up for it, after that, we could work on your magic."

"Really?" Fleur asked, almost squealing in delight.

"Really. I've been treating you like a general dogsbody. It's about time that changed."

Fleur did squeal this time. She also flung her arms around me in a great big hug and bounced me up and down.

CHAPTER THIRTEEN

"Right. What have we got?" I said, clapping my hands and delving into the pantry. "Potatoes, carrots, cauliflower. I think I also have some petit pois in the freezer. That's the veggie side sorted. I have flour, eggs, and milk, so we can whip up a batch of Yorkshire puds if you fancy."

Fleur looked at me a little wide-eyed and shrugged. "I'm good with whatever you'd like."

"If there's anything you don't like, just tell me," I said and moved to open the freezer and see what we had on the meat side of things. "Time got away from me, so I haven't defrosted anything, but I have a pre-packed honey-glazed gammon joint we could have that cooks from frozen, or there are some beef cubes. We could always make a beef and onion pie."

"Pie sounds good." Abby jumped up on the counter next to Fleur and nudged her. Fleur patted her on the head and Abby nuzzled in closer.

"She senses your unease," I said and smiled at the cat.

Although we'd agreed for Fleur to keep the cat, I hadn't broached the idea I'd fermented in my brain after their first day together. A part of me wondered if there was still a chance Benjamin or Trisha would claim Abby, but given that they hadn't shown the slightest interest in her whereabouts or wellbeing, I wouldn't hand her over to them now, even if they tried. No. I'd pretty much made up my mind that Abby was to be Fleur's familiar. It was just with everything going on I hadn't discussed the idea with them yet. Niles rubbed against my leg and I leaned over to give him a long body stroke. He knew my plans.

"I-I like all the food," Fleur said with a note of worry in her voice. "I just don't know how to go about cooking any of it."

"Well, that's the first place we can start with your training, then. Cooking, whether a hearty meal or a magical spell, is practically the same thing. You need good ingredients, good intentions, and a confident hand."

Fleur grimaced. "I can muster the 'good' parts. I'm just not so sure about the confident part."

I grabbed a few potatoes and placed them on a chopping board on the centre island. "Give them a wash and remove the skin with this," I said, handing Fleur a peeler. When she looked at me blankly, I mimed how to use it and placed a saucepan on the counter next to her. "Chuck them in here when you're done."

Fleur lifted the board and took the potatoes closer to the sink to wash them while I started on the other vegetables. It was nice having her in the kitchen with me while we worked. It reminded me of when I was little, and I used to help my mum. I'd trim the Brussels sprouts while she pottered away preparing everything else. I probably held the same goofy look of concentration on my face that Fleur did now.

"Was your mum not much of a cook?" I asked, while cutting the leaves from the cauliflower head. Then instantly regretted asking when Fleur's face fell. Only then did I remember her saying her parents were both gone. "I'm sorry. I shouldn't pry," I said, and focused on the task at hand.

Fleur placed her second peeled potato in the pan and sighed. "It's fine. You've done so much for me—"

"I haven't done a lot, and even if I had, you're under no obligation to tell me about your past," I said, even though I was curious. My relationship with my dad was bad or maybe non-existent would be the better term these days, but mum... mum had been an angel. At least, that's what she seemed in my memories.

"The truth is, I never really knew my mum or my dad. For all I know, she might not have known who he was. I was in foster homes by the time I was two. I bounced around different homes after that."

"Aren't you still young enough to come under the care of the council?" I asked. I didn't add that I thought part of a carer's role was to make sure their foster kids were prepared for independent living. Which meant cooking, cleaning, and laundry, amongst other things.

"Assuming your foster carer agrees, you can stay with them until you're 21. Mine didn't," she added, and a sad twitch formed at the corner of her lip. "As far as the council goes, they assign you an adviser and make a 'pathway plan'." The last part was said with sarcasm and accompanied by air quotation marks. To say that Fleur wasn't impressed with her plan might be an understatement.

She fell silent after that, and when she finished the potatoes, I showed her what to do next and set her up with a rolling pin and a block of pre-made pastry. I may enjoy cooking and believe it's a valuable life skill everyone should possess, but that didn't mean I was above cutting corners when needed.

When we'd finished, and everything was in the oven, I took Fleur to my snug. The cats accompanied us. She gaped at all the jars lining the shelves of the apothecary cabinets and asked if she could look.

"Of course," I said, "that's why we're here."

Fleur trailed her finger along the edge of one shelf as though she wanted to touch all the bottles but was afraid to. Her hand froze on a couple of bottles pushed to one side. "Lavender, helichrysum, and frankincense," she said, tilting her head to read the labels. "All the others are in alphabetical order. Why aren't these?"

I scrunched up my nose. "Mostly because I've been a little lazy and haven't made time to put them in their proper place." I frowned as I remembered lining them up on the worktable along with copaiba oil. Niles had assessed each oil before settling on the copaiba for the remedy I'd delivered to Mrs Jenkins' house. I said as much to Fleur and explained how choosing the right oil and enhancing any beneficial properties within it is less time-consuming than creating something from scratch. "Plus," I added with a pointed look, "if some inquisitive customer looks at the property of the oil on the internet, it will align with the properties I claimed it possessed. That's why I wanted you to read everything on my site. Knowing the holistic properties of everything will help you with your magic."

Fleur smiled and shook her head. "My magic," she said with a note of disbelief. "It's funny hearing you say that."

"It's even more fun to do it," I said and decided to give her a spot test. I lifted my hand and pointed it at the first oil not sitting in its allotted place. "Frankincense," I said as it floated through the air and slotted intself in between the fir and galangal oil while Fleur gawped. "Do you remember what that's good for?"

"Stress and negative emotions," Fleur answered, her voice soft.

"That's right. It's non-toxic to cats and can also help boost the immune system as well as improve sleep. How about this one?" I smiled and floated the second bottle in front of her face and deposited it between the laurus nobilis and ledum.

"Lavender's good for stress and anxiety," Fleur said, a bit more sure of her answer this time.

"Yep. Can you think of anything else?"

"Acne and joint pain."

I nodded. This time instead of using my magic to lift the third bottle, I picked it up and placed it on the worktable in the centre of the room before walking and indicating the spot on the shelf between the henna oil and the hickory nut oil. "Your turn," I said. "The helichrysum belongs here. Amongst other things, it's good for coughs, colds, and several digestive issues. I want you to do the same as you did with the Sherbet lemon, but this time, don't concentrate so hard on what you're trying to achieve. Remember the way the magic felt on the roof? Let it flow through you. Open your mind and believe. Don't try to move it, just picture it already going where you need it to."

Fleur took a deep breath and stared at the bottle.

"You're thinking too much," I said.

"It's hard not to."

I brushed away her comment with my hand. "You're a teenager. You can go days without thinking at all, " I said in jest.

Fleur rolled her eyes and moved her pointed finger closer to the bottle. Abby jumped up on the counter next to it and nudged her hand. "Not now, baby," Fleur said and pushed the cat to the side a little.

"She can sense you're thinking too much. Let her help. Instead of pointing your finger at the bottle as though trying to shoot a laser beam through it, why don't you give her a pet, imagine what you need to happen, and the second you have it fully in your mind, swoosh your finger at the bottle and make it happen."

Fleur rolled her shoulder and shook out the tension from her arm. She stroked Abby once on the head and closed her eyes. The cat nuzzled Fleur's hand with her nose and flipped it over her head, repeating the motion until Fleur needed no further instruction and continued the stroking motion naturally. After a minute or so, she opened her eyes and flicked her hand at the bottle. It darted across the room towards the shelf at a hundred miles an hour. With a fraction of a second to spare, I twitched my hand and stopped it from smashing into the other bottles.

Fleur winced. "Sorry," she said and rubbed the back of her neck.

"For what? You did it, and without breaking a sweat, I might add."

Fleur looked at the bottle, and a wide smile split her face. "I actually did. I can't believe I did it."

"Believe it," I said and wondered, without voicing, if her mother could have been a witch. It was the only way I could explain the well of power I felt open inside her.

We spent the rest of the day helping Fleur practice control, eating dinner, and vegging in front of the TV. When night-time fell, Fleur headed back to her flat with Abby in tow, and I settled into bed with Niles.

"I think they're made for each other," I said to Niles as he purred on my chest. "I wonder if it was fate that I found Tanya's body and led me to the cat. Maybe the powers that be knew Fleur would need a familiar and sent us her perfect companion."

Niles blinked in response, and I closed my eyes. Within minutes, I'd drifted off to sleep.

It was pitch black in the room when the bedside phone rang. I groaned at the noise, squinted in the meagre light, and noted the bedside clock reading a little after midnight.

I fumbled for the phone. "Hello," I said, my voice groggy from sleep.

"Eira. It's Aaron. Mum's missing."

"What?" I shot up in the bed. "What do you mean, missing?"

"She phoned earlier, upset. I've been at her house all evening and she's still not home. I've phoned everyone. What the hell did you say to her?"

"Nothing that would cause her to disappear! Stay where you are. I'm on my way."

I'd had such a fun, relaxing day with Fleur, and had almost forgotten my encounter with Mrs Jenkins. Worry tightened my stomach. I honestly didn't like the woman, but I hated the thought of anything bad happening to her.

CHAPTER FOURTEEN

Aaron was waiting on the doorstep, silhouetted by the porch light, when I arrived at his mother's house.

"Any news?" I asked, although the answer was obvious.

His face looked like thunder when he stepped out of the shadows, his fists clenched. "I should have listened when she told me to stay away from you."

I bristled, but knew his anger stemmed from his worry about his mum. "I doubt her disappearance has anything to do with me." I'd had a chance to ponder my last discussion with Mrs Jenkins on the walk over. If it had spurred her upset call to Aaron, then it had to be about her imprisoning Abby. She was guilty. I knew it in my gut. Not that I'd tell Aaron. "Where have you looked?" I asked instead.

"I've called all her friends. Not one of them has seen her."

I huffed out a breath and looked around. "Have you spoken to any of the neighbours?" I asked, unable to stop my eyes flickering to Tanya's house. It stood in complete darkness. No alarm bells sounded in my head and the feeling of compressed anguish that circled it when I found her body had dissipated. It looked no different from any other house on the street, apart from the absence of lights.

Before Aaron had the chance to answer, a car pulled up and parked in front of the drive. Kate hopped out.

"I got your message," she said, joining us in front of the garage. I'd sent her a quick text before leaving the house. She had told me to keep her updated with my whereabouts, and although I wasn't sure if that still stood, I didn't think it would hurt her to know Mrs Jenkins was missing. She nodded to me, not waiting for a response, before turning her attention to Aaron. "What makes you think your mother is missing?" she asked.

He glared at me. "She phoned this morning, upset. She wasn't happy I'd spent time with Eira when she'd forbidden me from doing so."

I wanted to tell him he was a grown man in his forties and not a five-year-old child, but something told me that wouldn't go down well. Not now, or possibly ever, for that matter.

"Whilst I understand your mother was upset about you going against her wishes, that doesn't explain—"

"She was crying. My mother is not a woman prone to bouts of tears. I told her I was on my way. She muttered that she should never have agreed to hand over the cat and hung up. That was a little after ten this morning. I'd arrived to find her missing by half-past."

Kate glanced at me and sighed. "I hate to ask you this," she said to Aaron, "but we believe your mother may have stolen your neighbour's cat. Who—"

"Impossible. She's allergic." He almost growled his response. "Why would you think that?" Kate's eyes flicked to me again. Aaron must have noticed as his followed suit. "You," he said and stepped forward, looking as if he might punch me. "If anything has happened to her, I'll kill..."

Kate stepped between us and cleared her throat. "Threats to kill carry a sentence of ten years, Mr Jenkins. Are you sure you want to finish that statement? Now, as your mother said that she should never have agreed to hand over the cat, that implies she took it and passed it on to someone else. Would you have any idea who that might be?"

"This is ridiculous. My mother is missing and all you want to do is throw around wild accusations."

"Aaron," I said. "It might help us find her. You have to ask yourself why she bought the oil."

The look he flashed me could freeze lava. "Leave," he said. "I binned that oil yesterday. I wish I'd never laid eyes on it or you. You've done enough damage. It would have been better for everyone if you'd never moved to the village."

My chest tightened and once again I tried to tell myself that his anger stemmed from his worry, but I realised that didn't matter. The fact was, I had accused his mum of catnapping, and I was right, but now she was missing. I wanted to feel some sense of loss at him pushing me away, but I wasn't sure you could lose something that never was. Mostly, I felt a sense of relief. The last thing I needed was a relationship with a mummy's boy. A forty-five-year-old mummy's boy at that, and one with a temper. A temper, the magical soothing oil had dampened during our previous meetings. I sighed and turned to leave.

"Eira, I don't want you walking home alone," Kate called after me. "Wait in the car and I'll drive you."

I sat in the passenger seat and tried to keep my eyes forward, but every so often they drifted towards Kate and Aaron. Whenever they did, I noticed Aaron's icy stare. If it wasn't obvious that he knew nothing about his mother keeping the cat, I would think him a possible suspect in Tanya's murder. Although, as I thought about it, I realised it could have been him.

He sure looked like he'd push me down the stairs for his mother. I scoffed and shook my head. Until now, I'd have believed Mrs Jenkins was the more capable of murder out of the two.

The car door opened, breaking my train of thought. "What are you going to do to find Mrs Jenkins?" I asked.

"Try to reach her by phone. There's a possibility she's just avoiding her son. Check hospital admissions, that sort of thing. If that fails, I'll see if we can trace her mobile phone and the calls made from it."

I nodded, afraid to ask my next question, but I couldn't avoid the answer forever. "Is it my fault she's missing?" I asked, and Kate sighed.

"Why? Is there something you'd like to confess?" she asked in an echo of the question she asked me the first time we met.

I turned to see if she was serious and found a slight smile playing at the edge of her lips. I smiled back. "Thank you," I said.

"Nothing to thank me for," she answered, but we both knew there was. By her simple actions, Kate had let me off the hook. I'd had nothing to do with Tanya's murder and nothing to do with Abby's catnapping. As Mrs Jenkins' disappearance had to do with either one or both of these things, then it wasn't my fault. No matter how much Aaron wanted to blame me.

I risked a glance back at the house as Kate started the car and pulled away. The front door was closed, and Aaron was nowhere to be seen. The porch light flicked off, and the house became as dark as Tanya's. Something clicked inside my head at the thought. I'd been so ready to consider everyone a suspect in Tanya's murder, but had overlooked the person geographically closest to her. Why?

"Sorry?" Kate said, and I realised I'd spoken my thoughts out loud.

"Mrs Jenkins could have killed Tanya," I said. "She had her cat. Why couldn't she be guilty of both crimes?"

"Mainly because she has an alibi," Kate said, and turned into the one-way system and the road leading to my cottage.

"Oh." I sighed and turned to look out the window. So much for that idea.

The houses went by in a blur of darkness and streetlights. Given the hour, the roads were silent apart from the soft whirr of our car's engine and the tyres on the tarmac. I suddenly felt very tired, but I worried I wouldn't sleep without knowing that Mrs Jenkins was safe.

"Here you go," Kate said, and pulled up outside my cottage. "I'll send a car around to check up on you throughout the night."

"Thanks," I said and got out of the car. Before I closed the door, I leaned down and asked Kate to let me know if she found Mrs Jenkins.

She agreed. "But no more meddling," she said.

I gave a wry laugh. "No more meddling. Detective work is best left with the detective," I said. "I would never have thought to check if Mrs Jenkins had an alibi."

This time, Kate laughed. "Actually, I didn't," she said and huffed out a breath. "Trisha Baxter, Tanya's sister, was with her from nine Wednesday morning until four in the afternoon. They alibi each other."

I said goodbye and was about to close the door when something struck me. Instead, I jumped back in the car.

"No, they don't." I said, much to Kate's confusion. "Mrs Jenkins was in the store by herself for a good forty minutes Wednesday lunchtime. I remember the time because I'd just heated a tin of soup for dinner. I sold her an allergy remedy and a smoke-cleansing kit. She had no idea what it was for, but was intrigued by the packaging. I took her through the contents one by one and explained how to use it. It was as she left that she asked me to deliver a cat-soothing remedy to her home that evening. I had to reheat my soup when she left."

"What time was this?" Kate asked.

"A quarter to one. It must have been almost half-past when she left. She doesn't have an alibi at all. She could have easily made it back to her house before two and killed Tanya."

Kate leaned her head back on the chair rest and closed her eyes. "It also means Trisha Baxter doesn't have an alibi, either."

I raised my eyebrows and looked at Kate. She must have sensed me staring as she opened her eyes and glared at me. "I wonder why they would both lie," I said.

"You got any coffee in that house of yours?" Kate asked, laughing. "I have a feeling it's going to be a long night."

"I have coffee, but I can do you one better." I smiled and opened my door again. "I have ginseng tea."

CHAPTER FIFTEEN

Kate made a few calls and drank the offered tea. "You were right," she said as soon as she'd finished. "This stuff is better than coffee. I feel as though I've had a full eight hours' sleep."

I smiled. Magically infused tea would do that for you. I just wished it would do the same for me. In contrast, I felt as though I'd had around three hours' sleep. Still, it was better than none.

"What happens now?" I asked, rinsing my empty cup and placing it to drain.

Kate checked the time on her phone. "Officer Johnson is calling the hospital to see if Mrs Jenkins has been admitted. He'll meet me at Trisha Baxter's house in the morning. Until then, I'll go home. I would have grabbed some sleep, but thanks to your tea, I'm not sleepy anymore. But a shower wouldn't go amiss." She smiled and handed me her empty mug, which I washed and placed with mine.

"Stay out of trouble," she said and turned to leave.

"Trust me, I plan on doing just that."

As soon as she'd left, I sat in front of the TV and switched on the news. The reporter analysed the rise in food bank use in recent years, which made me depressed, so I muted the sound and closed my eyes. Niles curled up my lap and I must have drifted off to sleep as bright sunlight was streaming through the windows when I awoke to banging on the back door.

"Morning," Fleur said as soon as I opened it. She was dressed in her signature tights and boots, but this time she wore a green sweater and a tartan skirt. As always, her make-up was flawless and today she'd created a cat-eye liner look. Abby brushed past me and into the kitchen. "Did we wake you?" Fleur asked.

"It's fine," I said, and ushered her into the kitchen with the offer of some tea and toast.

As we ate at the breakfast bar, I told her everything that had happened during the night.

"Which one of them killed Tanya?" she asked. "David, Trisha or Mrs Jenkins?"

"I haven't got a clue. I'm ready for this whole mess to

be over, if I'm honest. We're running around here, there and everywhere, and solving nothing." I felt a little melancholic about everything. My one and only customer was a racist, a catnapper, and possibly a murderer. Aaron was her son and now hated me, and I'd neglected my business for days. To top it all off, the more I thought about Benjamin, the more guilty I felt. He was just a kid, and I'd treated him badly. He was going through a rough time and heaven knew how he'd pay for his mother's funeral. The only good thing to come into my life was Fleur, and possibly Kate and Susan. But I wasn't sure I'd see either of them again after the case was over. "I need to focus on the business today," I said. "We can leave everything else to the police."

"I've been thinking about the business," Fleur said and popped a piece of toast in her mouth. "You probably don't remember, but the first order I placed with you was for a crystal pack. I saw one of your ads on Facebook, offering a free pack for the price of postage."

"I remember," I said. "It's how I get a lot of my new customers."

Fleur nodded and waved her half-eaten toast at me. "What did you do to get customers through the door of the store?" she asked.

I had to confess that I hadn't done anything. Selling online, I'd done everything I could to get eyes on my business, but in the physical world, I'd assumed people would walk in off the street. "What do you have in mind?" I asked.

Fleur jumped down from her stool and tossed her toast onto her plate. "How about a grand opening party?" she said, making a dramatic arch with her hands. "We could have tea and cake and give out little samples of oil and stuff. As soon as people feel the benefits of your spells, they'll be back."

I smiled, my mood lifting. "That's a great idea. We could close the store while we prepare. Do you think we have time to plan everything before Friday?"

"Sure, we do." Fleur squealed and pulled me from my perch. "This is going to be awesome," she said, and I couldn't help but smile at her enthusiasm. Maybe it would be.

We closed the shop and put a big sign in the window advertising a grand opening on Friday at 6 p.m. Refreshments would be provided, and samples supplied. I called around a couple of caterers and found one who could provide a simple, sweet buffet menu at short notice, and Fleur placed an ad in the paper and in some local Facebook groups.

"I think we're good to go," I said and glanced at the clock. It was almost lunchtime. I didn't feel like cooking, so I suggested we go to the café for lunch.

"We could ask to put a flyer up in the café if they have a board," Fleur suggested. "It would only take a few minutes to whip one up on the computer." I agreed, and Fleur worked her technical magic to create something that looked both professional and eye-catching.

The manager of the café was more than happy to oblige our request and said she'd been meaning to check out the store and would be along herself on Friday. She also gave us the ten percent discount she reserved for locals on our baguettes. The day was shaping up quite nicely until my phone rang while we were eating.

"Hello," I said, answering the call. "What do you want?" I'd tried not to think of Mrs Jenkins or Tanya's murder and all the possible suspects all morning, and with Fleur keeping me enthused and busy, I'd succeeded, but at the sound of Aaron's voice, my melancholy flooded back.

"My mother is still missing," he said. "I hope you're proud of yourself."

"Aaron... I—"

"You're what? Sorry? You're an attention seeking lunatic. What if my mum did take the stupid cat? Maybe she was right to. Did you ever think about that? Tanya's been nothing but a disgrace and an embarrassment to her family. The cat was better off without her."

Fleur reached across the table and touched my hand. A concerned look flashed across her face. 'What's he saying?' she mouthed.

I pulled the phone away and relayed what Aaron had said. She scrunched up her face, snatched the phone from my hand, and ended the call.

"You don't have to take any crap from him or anyone else," she said.

I gave her a half grin. She was right, but that didn't make life any easier.

We finished our food, and when we left, my eye caught the flyers advertising the various businesses on the fence surrounding the scaffolding on the derelict building. It felt like aeons ago that Fleur and I had broken inside and climbed to the roof. I wondered what the council workers had decided to do, but shook the thought from my head when I realised they weren't due to call until later today.

It was then I remembered what Fleur had said on the roof about jumping to conclusions. The cat-soothing copaiba oil had taken the edge off Aaron's naturally tempestuous nature. He'd looked about ready to kill me for his mum. Could he have killed Tanya? Fleur was right when she said how quickly he'd ingratiated himself into my life, and truth be told, he'd instigated every step of my investigation from going to see Benjamin, to Trisha, and Susan. I sighed and looked at my feet. I was back to the fact that he couldn't have thrown the bricks at himself and he couldn't have set the fires at my house.

Fleur nudged me with her elbow. "We could make more flyers and post them around the town," she said.

I tried to regain my previous good mood and smiled. "Good idea."

Despite my words, Fleur must have sensed I wanted to be alone as she offered to walk around the village and post the flyers by herself. I thanked her and considered getting some sleep.

I tossed and turned for a good hour, but Aaron's handsome face kept popping into my mind. I hated that he'd had gotten under my skin and I'd allowed his call to spoil my day, but I hated even more that I'd been an idiot to think him a good person in the first place, regardless of the effects of the oil. I should have known better after Chris and after discovering what his mum was really like. The apple doesn't fall far from the tree, as they say. When sleep proved elusive, I printed off a few more flyers and ventured outside.

I'd been meaning to buy a car. Chris and I had only had the one, and that was in his name, so it wasn't part of the property I'd claimed when I'd left. Instead, I'd rented a van to move all my things and vowed to get one when I'd settled. With the shop closed until Friday, I decided to find time to look for one this week. In the meantime, I pulled my bike out of the shed and hopped on top. After a slightly shaky start, I soon found my pace and set off around the village. When I spotted Fleur's flyer on the board in the common, I turned around so as not to trace her route and headed off on a side street in a different direction.

The cool heat of the afternoon warmed my back. The odd car drove by and an old man walked in the opposite direction on the pavement. He smiled and nodded his head at me in greeting when our eyes met. "Nice day for a ride," he said.

"That it is," I agreed and carried on my way.

After a while, I saw the gated entrance to the old university site. Inside a hut with a large glass window, a security guard alternated between watching the road and some monitors. He saw me looking at him and nodded his head in greeting. I nodded back, and an impulse overtook me. I wanted to see inside.

I cycled a little way back up the road and stashed my bike in some hedges before walking back, searching for another way onto the grounds. When I failed to find one, I went back to the gated area and glanced around. The security guard had made himself a cup of tea and was sipping it while looking at his wall of screens. With no one else around, I risked a little magic and nudged the bottom of the cup. I felt a little guilty when the hot liquid sploshed all over his uniform and he jumped from his seat, cursing. But not guilty enough not to take advantage of him darting out of view to clean himself up. I slipped inside the grounds and rushed towards the built-up area.

The campus was much bigger than I'd expected, and the main building was a treasure of architecture. It had to be more than a hundred years old. There were three floors and a stunning clock tower in the centre of the building. The surrounding area was full of modern glass extensions. I could have spent hours walking around the site, listening to the crickets and the birds and watching the bushes swaying in the breeze. Eventually, I came to what had to be the halls of residence.

I sat on the wall opposite and stared at the simple structures. It was eerie in the quiet with no one around and the sound of traffic diminished to a faraway hum. I wanted to imagine the way it had once been, full of students and life. Kate was right. It was a shame the place had closed.

I'd resolved to call it a day and head home when movement caught my eye between two of the buildings. I stood prepared for a telling off from a security guard, but when no one materialised, I wondered why and decided to investigate. I walked over, glancing at the buildings and trying to act as though I hadn't seen anything.

A man stepped out from the small walkway between the buildings. He looked to be in his late forties. He was clean, but unshaven, and his clothes were a little rumpled. There was a heaviness to the way he carried himself, as if something weighed him down.

"I'm guessing you're not meant to be here in much the same way I'm not," he said in a voice devoid of any regional accent.

"I guess not," I replied and readied my magic, just in case. "I'll tell you why I'm here, if you tell me why you are."

He glanced at the student hall to the right of him. "I'm here to say goodbye," he said.

I took another tentative step toward him. "Goodbye? Are you going anywhere nice?"

His dark eyes turned serious. "Yeah, I am," he said with a grim twist to his mouth. "I've got a job in Canada. I leave at the end of next week."

I followed his gaze. It froze on the end window of the top floor. From the look on his face, I hazarded a guess and said, "Congratulations, David," while my mind worked overtime. His leaving the country might explain why he took until now to kill Tanya, but somehow, I didn't think that was the case. I might be the worst judge of character in the history of the world, but the man before me seemed sad, more than murderous.

He turned his attention back to me and squinted his eyes. "Have we met before?" he asked.

"No, but I know some people who are looking for you."

He rubbed the back of his head. "I've probably caused a lot of worry with my disappearing act," he said. "I only meant to come for a few hours, but after I got here, I couldn't bring myself to leave again. It's hard, knowing I'll never return." He stepped out from the shadows and walked toward me. "Did Tanya guess where to find me?" he asked. "It would be just like her to send someone else than come herself. She hates this place."

I sighed and shook my head. "I'm very sorry to have to tell you this, but Tanya's dead." His face fell and tears welled in his eyes. He scrubbed them away with a rough hand. "I had thought there was a possibility you killed her," I continued. His face turned to shocked outrage, but I stopped him speaking by raising my hand. "I don't think that anymore," I added.

"What the hell happened?" he asked.

"Someone pushed her down the stairs."

"*Bleep!*" He sat on the ground and rubbed a hand over his head. I walked over and joined him. "What are you, the police?" he asked.

"No. I'm just a concerned friend."

He nodded. "She tell you about this place?" he asked.

"About Julie, you mean?"

"Yeah. Julie. I guess with Tanya gone, I can close the book on my past once and for all," he said in a monotone voice, his shoulders slumped. "That's what this entire trip was about. But *bleep*, I never thought it would end like this."

We sat in silence for a while. David was obviously working

through some complex emotions, and I wasn't sure how to help him. In truth, I wasn't sure what to do about the whole situation. I *should* call Kate, but the last thing he needed was to be dragged in for questioning.

"I came here first," he said, breaking the silence. "Attended the university. They were good times. Julie only chose the place for her course because of the stories I told her. I come back every year, sometimes more than once, wondering if I'll catch a glimpse of her ghost roaming the campus."

"Have you?" I asked.

David gave an incredulous laugh and shook his head. "Nah. I thought I saw Big Bertha once, though. All six-foot of her in her brown overalls and her hair tied back in a tight bun." He nodded towards the main building. "Through one of the windows on the ground floor." His face dropped. "She was found at the bottom of the stairs in '62. Before my time. But there were always stories and speculation as to whether or not she was pushed."

I sighed, not bothering to mention the similarities between Tanya's death and Big Bertha's. "We should leave," I said and glanced around. The sun cast long shadows over the ground and a chill breeze caused goosebumps to rise on my arm. "You can come to my house and let whoever needs to know that you're okay."

"Yeah." David stood, dusted himself off, and turned to Julie's window. "I really believed there was a chance I might see her. This place is built on the site of a Roman burial ground. There have been loads of sightings. Not just of Bertha, but of centurions roaming the grounds as well."

I stood and patted him on the back. "My guess is that Julie knew she was loved and moved on to a better place."

"I hope so," he said and pointed back behind the building. "My car's that way."

With that, we turned away from the halls and walked away. David, for the last time. I really hoped he found peace in Canada and vowed to make a spell to ensure he would.

CHAPTER SIXTEEN

Things didn't go quite to plan after we reached my house. David made a few phone calls, and I sent Kate a text to let her know where I'd found him. I stressed that he was definitely not our killer, and he would be at my house if she needed to talk to him. It was silly to think that would be the end of that matter. She turned up at my door not twenty minutes later, accompanied by a couple of officers.

"Where is he?" she asked and pushed past me into the cottage without so much as a by your leave. Niles tensed on the sofa where, moments before, he'd been sleeping. He looked for all the world as if he were ready to attack. I had to walk over and pick him up to calm him down.

Kate and the officers barrelled through the cottage and found David coming down the stairs. He'd had a shower and changed clothes, intending to freshen up before heading out on the road back to London. If Kate had been ten minutes later, he would have already left.

"David Mosley?"

"Yes."

The officers with Kate flipped him around, pushed him against the wall, and secured his wrists with plasticuffs.

"Everything okay?" Fleur asked when she emerged from the kitchen with a nervous, wide-eyed expression on her face.

"You are under arrest on suspicion of murder. You do not have to say anything, but it may harm your defence if you do not mention when questioned something which you later rely on in court. Anything you do say may be given in evidence." Kate read David his rights, and the officers pushed him towards the front door.

"You're making a mistake," I said, following them out. "He's innocent."

Kate turned to face me sharply. "You don't know that."

"And you have nothing that proves he's guilty." Niles sensed my displeasure and wriggled in my arms. I kissed him on the head and shushed him. He stilled, but flashed a warning glare at

Kate.

She gave him a double-take before turning her attention back to me. "Eira, he's been hiding out at the location of his sister's murder since the day Tanya was killed."

"He just wanted to say goodbye before leaving for Canada." I glanced outside. The police were putting David in the back of their van. His face looked more resigned than shocked. "If you'd have been there and seen him. He didn't do this. He would never have hurt the only link he still had to his sister."

Kate sighed and shook her head in disbelief. "Can you hear what you're saying? He was planning to leave the country and cleaning up loose ends before doing so," she said and turned to leave.

"Kate," I called, and she froze in the doorway. "If he's the killer, why am I still alive? And the fire? He had no reason to set fire to my doors. It doesn't make any sense."

Her shoulders heaved, but she didn't turn around to face me. Instead, she carried on walking to her car.

"Oh, *bleeping bleep*!" I said and slammed my front door.

"Are you okay?" Fleur asked when I stomped into the living room. I glanced up and saw her try to wipe the slight smile from her face.

"What's so funny?" Fleur sucked in her lips and shrugged before staring at Niles as though pleading for help. "Well?" I asked, only feeling slightly guilty for my tone.

"I've just never heard anyone say bleeping bleep before," she said, and her smile returned, although she tried her best to hide it.

I gasped. "Did I really say that?" I drew my hand to cover my mouth. Behind it, a smile formed, and I bit my lip to stop it. "I can't believe I said that. I am so sorry."

Fleur's grin grew wider. "It's okay," she said. "It's not as if you actually swore."

"It's not the words that matter," I said. "It's the meaning behind them."

Fleur nodded and placed her hands on her hips in a mock-stern pose. "In that case, mind your language, young lady."

With the look on her face, I couldn't do anything but laugh. Fleur joined me. When we'd subsided, I placed Niles on the ground and linked arms with Fleur, suggesting we grab a cup of tea and figure out what we were going to do next.

CHAPTER SEVENTEEN

We called a solicitor to meet David at the police station and sat in the kitchen, unsure what our next move could be. I'd flicked the kettle on and grabbed a couple of mugs from the cupboard. Fleur's phone rang. She jumped to answer it with a smile on her face.

"Hi Alecia," she said, and I stepped into the living room to give her some privacy. It was nice to hear the excitement in her voice when she talked to her friend.

"No, don't worry about it. Everything's great. I've found an amazing place and a new job. Things are really going well." She fell silent for a few seconds, and then said, "I can't make it this

Friday."

My shoulders sagged, and I glanced at Niles, deciding I shouldn't eavesdrop anymore. He and Abby snuggled on the sofa a little distance apart.

"We've been monopolising Fleur's time," I said to the two of them, giving Niles a little nudge to shift over so I could squeeze in between them.

Once again, I realised how much I'd been taking advantage of Fleur. A week ago, I'd been one hundred percent self-reliant, and now I counted on her to wake me up in the morning, open the shop, and spend all her free time keeping me company. It wasn't right. I stared at the muted TV, stroked Niles and Abby on either side of me, and resolved to change. Fleur might be my apprentice, but that didn't give me the right to consume all her time with my drama. She needed to be out having fun with people her own age.

I settled there and then on giving her the rest of the week off, as well as Friday evening. I could give out free samples without her. As soon as she finished the call and entered the room, I said as much.

Fleur looked at me with her big wide eyes and perfect cheekbones. She truly was a very pretty girl and something of a contradiction. She could look and act so confident at times, and then seem scared of her own shadow at others. Now was one of those other times. She opened her mouth as if to say something, but then shrugged whatever the thought was away and nodded. "If you don't want me there, I understand," she said with a quiver in her voice.

I instantly realised I'd made a huge mistake.

"Goodness, no. Of course, I want you there," I said and jumped to my feet, much to the annoyance of both cats. "I just don't want you to miss out on a night out with your friends for a work thing."

Fleur smiled and bobbed on her feet. "You heard that?" she asked.

"Only a few words as I was leaving."

"I would like to be there on Friday," she said. "Just to see how things turn out."

"Well, it was your idea." I smiled and hoped she found it reassuring. "It's understandable you'd want to show your face, and with all the effort you've put in, I've no doubt the reopening will be a roaring success."

Fleur squealed. "I'm actually crazy excited about it. Thank you." She pulled her phone out of the pocket on her skirt and looked at it as though waiting for it to ring again. "My friend, Alecia, the one I told you about in Cwmbran, she mentioned the possibility of getting together now at The Ship. I'm not sure there's anything else we can do for David other than wait and see what happens. So, if it's okay with you, I wouldn't mind going out for a few hours to catch up... I wouldn't mention anything about magic or anything like that, I promise."

"No. Sorry. I didn't mean no, you can't go. No, I know you won't say anything about magic." I shook my head, realising I was babbling. "I mean, of course. That's brilliant. Go." I shooed her with my hand. "You don't need to ask me for permission. Have fun."

"Okay, great. I'll call her back and get ready." With that, Fleur turned on her heels and walked through the kitchen and out the back door to her flat. I couldn't imagine what she needed to do to get ready. She already looked immaculate.

I gave Niles a little shove again and sat between him and Abby on the sofa.

"It looks like it's just the three of us tonight." I noted a stray white hair had landed on my jeans. I stared at it for a moment, confused. I glanced from my perfect black bundle of fluff to Abby's white and black and smiled. "How do you guys feel about take-out? I'm thinking Chinese food or maybe Lebanese. A nice Shawarma would go down a treat and you could have some of the chicken."

My two feline companions ignored me, and I wasn't ready to move again just yet, so instead of ordering, I reached for the remote and turned on the TV. I must have flicked through every channel at least three times before deciding there was nothing I wanted to watch. I honestly didn't know why I paid for all the packages when there was never anything on. I was about to flick over when an advert with a little girl riding a bike flashed on the screen.

"My bike," I said, remembering I'd hidden it in the bushes before meeting David. We'd driven back to my place in his car, and I'd forgotten all about it.

I grabbed my jacket and headed out. It shouldn't take more than an hour to fetch my bike and return home. After that, I could order the Shawarma whether the cats fancied some or not.

I walked the dark streets and sucked in the fresh spring air. The sky was clear and, with the moon waning, the stars filled the velvet dark with their sparkling glory. The only sound was the gentle whisper of my breath and the pounding of my feet against the pavement.

I loved this time of day when the hustle and bustle had finished, and a quiet calm settled over everything. I was beginning to love this place, too. The history poured out of everything I looked at, from the Roman fortress and baths to the museum and amphitheatre. The Priory hotel on the main street used to be a monastery dating back to the 12th century. I even remembered reading somewhere that Tennyson lodged in the Hanbury Arms and looked out over the River Usk when he wrote about King Arthur and Guinevere in *Idylls of the King*. Mum used to read the poems to me. "For man is man and master of his fate." That always stuck in my head for some reason, especially after she died, and I was shipped off to Swansea to live with a father who neither liked me nor wanted me. I'd never felt much in control of my own fate then.

I shook the thought from my head and approached the bushes where I'd hidden my bike. A small smile spread across my face when I found that no one had discovered it and taken it for their own. After a little wrestling with some entangled branches, I dragged it free and dusted off the leaves and mud that had adhered themselves to the frame.

I sighed, about to climb on, but froze for a few minutes and stared into the distance at the dark area that encompassed the deserted campus. This was the place where everything began for David, but when I got on my bike and headed to The Hawthorns estate where Tanya and Mrs Jenkins both lived, I realised that there was where everything had started for me. I couldn't say why, but I felt a pull to be there now.

Ten minutes later, I rounded the bend in the road and entered the cul-de-sac. Mrs Jenkins' house was engulfed in complete darkness. Aaron's car was no longer parked in the drive. I'd half expected to find him waiting at the house for his mother to come home. I have to admit to a sense of relief that I wouldn't have to deal with him.

I propped my bike against the wall and turned my attention to Tanya's house. David hadn't killed her. I was certain of that, but who did?

My thoughts drifted to the first time I'd spoken to Kate. I'd thrown out a comment about someone coming to collect the reward for Abby and Tanya not having the money. Of course, I didn't know how right I'd been about her not having any money at the time.

I huffed out a breath and entered the garden, squeezing through a narrow walkway and around the back to survey the entire house. I found a conservatory extension and looked through the windows. The only things inside were a set of armchairs on either side of a stereo system and a picture of the forest hanging on the wall. The doors leading into the main part of the house were shuttered, and I couldn't see through to the room. Not that I knew what I was looking for.

The house was in a good state of repair and the chairs were a classic wingback and looked expensive, but looks can be deceiving. Trisha's house was pristine with expensive furnishings, but upon closer inspection, they'd all shown a slight fading to their colour. Maybe Tanya's was the same.

Mrs Jenkins may not be my favourite person, but I couldn't believe she'd kill Tanya over some reward money. But she had catnapped Abby. Her comment to Aaron had proved that.

I felt no closer to finding Tanya's killer than I had when I'd first started investigating. It could be Aaron, Mrs Jenkins, Trisha, her husband, Susan... It could be countless other people I've never even met or considered.

I rubbed my head and tried to order my thoughts. Something about Mrs Jenkins' comment to Aaron triggered a memory. An image of me on the sofa with Niles and Abby on either side flashed through my mind. The white hair on my jeans. I'd found a white hair on my lap at Trisha's house too. At the time, I assumed I must have brought it with me, but what if I didn't? Mrs Jenkins hadn't kept Abby; she'd handed her to someone, that's what Aaron had said.

A car alarm sounded in the distance and a dog barked, making me jump and decide it was time to leave. I didn't know why I'd been drawn to come to the house. Some master of my own fate, I was. I vowed to go home, order my food, and figure out my next step.

When I neared the end of the narrow passage between the houses, leading to the front, a shuffle sounded behind me. I turned to face the way I'd come and glimpsed a figure in the darkness, but couldn't make out a face. My heart raced. I lifted my hand, ready to use magic should I need to, when a second noise sounded from the opposite direction. I whipped my head around to look and glimpsed the underside of a pan as it smashed into my head.

I crumpled to the ground as blackness overtook me.

CHAPTER EIGHTEEN

Light flickered at the edge of my consciousness. My head throbbed, my mouth was parched, and my body ached. I tried to move, but my arms were tied behind my back. I blinked my vision into focus and discovered I was in a room, bound to a dining chair. From the shutters covering the far wall, I guessed I was in Tanya's house.

I tried to flick my fingers to use my magic and failed. My bonds were too tight. I wriggled, attempting to get free, but only succeeded in hurting my wrists. My mother had been able to use her powers without moving a muscle. With no one to teach me how, I'd never mastered that technique.

I gathered my magic. A channel opened, and I sensed it drift around me. I took a deep breath, drawing it inside, but when I pictured it breaking my bonds, nothing happened. *"Bleep!"* I said and vowed that if I ever got out of this mess, I'd practice using magic without the use of my hands until it became second nature.

Muffled voices sounded in the house. I strained to hear what they were saying. It was impossible to make out the words, but I did note they both belonged to women. I felt a little giddy at the realisation, relief that neither could be Aaron.

I took a deep breath and decided that as I needed to buy time, there was no harm in letting my captors know I was awake.

"Hey," I shouted, and decided to hazard a guess. "Trisha. I know it's you and Mrs Jenkins. You too. You're not going to get away with this."

The door banged open and Trisha stepped inside, brandishing a cast iron pan. Rage blazed in her eyes. "Shut up," she said.

I raised my eyebrows. If she'd wanted me to stay quiet, she should have gagged me.

Mrs Jenkins entered behind Trisha. She pushed her glasses up on her face and looked anywhere but directly at me. "We should have let her leave," she said and pulled on Trisha's arm, pulling the pan to her side. "I don't want any trouble." Her round face looked frightened, as if she couldn't believe what was happening.

"She brought this on herself, snooping around and spreading rumours. She should have minded her own business and left things alone."

"Now, she'll go to the police."

"You should have thought about that after deciding to leave Tanya's front door open for her to find."

My eyebrows raised at that revelation. They'd planned for me to find her body, but why order the cat oil? Unless it was an attempt to cover their taking the cat.

Trisha huffed out a breath and lifted the pan again. "She won't be able to go anywhere."

"What do you mean? We can't keep her tied up forever," Mrs Jenkins said. Trisha didn't respond. Instead, she glared at me with an intensity that promised violence.

I exhaled slowly and shook my head. "She means I'll be dead. Didn't she tell you? That's how she deals with all her problems." I narrowed my eyes at Trisha and willed her to confess.

"What?" Mrs Jenkins' voice held a note of panic. She looked at me for the first time and rushed forward. She dropped to a crouch in front of me and placed her hands on my knees. "You've got it all wrong. I took Abby. You were right about that, but only to teach Tanya a lesson. It was only going to be for a few more days. But she fell. It was an accident."

As she babbled, my eyes never left Trisha's. I could almost feel sorry for Mrs Jenkins. It was clear she believed every word she said, almost as clear as Trisha being a stone-cold killer. Watching her now, it was hard to imagine her deferring to her husband and his old-fashioned ideas.

I closed my eyes and nodded my head slowly. Of course. "You're a racist," I said, opening my eyes and turning my attention to Mrs Jenkins. "Aaron called it an old-fashioned idea. I called it discrimination and prejudice."

Mrs Jenkins spluttered and looked at me, confused. I shifted my attention back to Trisha. She hadn't moved. Her heels were of a sensible height and her shirt buttoned all the way up to her neck; even her arms were covered.

"I was told your husband also has old-fashioned ideas," I said to her. "That's why you murdered Julie. You couldn't have your sister in a lesbian relationship and embarrassing the family."

Mrs Jenkins swivelled her head. "What's she talking about? Who's Julie?"

"Julie was the love of Tanya's life," I answered on Trisha's behalf. "Why couldn't you be happy for her?"

"Because she always spoiled everything," Trisha said, speaking for the first time. "She had to steal my best friend. The first one I'd made away from her influence, and then... what they did was unthinkable. I begged her to end their relationship. She refused. She said if Tim really loved me, then it wouldn't matter who she dated."

Her words made me feel sick to my stomach. Tanya knew her sister had killed Julie. All these years, she'd lived with the knowledge. That's what she meant when she'd told Julie she knew and did nothing. "She was going to tell David," I said. He was leaving for the last time, and she wanted him to know the truth. "That's why you killed her. But why did you try to kill Aaron?"

Mrs Jenkins gasped. Her mouth fell open. "Aaron? My Aaron?"

"He was as bad as Tanya." Trisha almost spat the words. "An embarrassment to your good name. He once told Tanya he loved her, but her body wasn't even cold before he moved on to this tart."

Mrs Jenkins looked from me to Trisha and back again. She scrambled around to the back of the chair and fumbled to undo my ropes. She wasn't quick enough. Trisha rushed forward and whacked her on the head with the pan.

I strained in my seat, trying to see Mrs Jenkins. Her head was out of view, but a gentle stirring of her chest showed she still breathed.

"You're never going to get away with this," I said, turning my attention back to Trisha, my voice calm.

She smiled and raised the pan above my head.

Glass shattered.

She froze.

I turned my head to the sound.

A fraction of a second later, the shutters leading to the conservatory blasted from their hinges. Niles, in full glorious panther form, burst into the room.

Terror flooded Trisha's eyes.

Niles took one look at me and swiped at the ropes binding my hands with his claws before turning his attention to my captor. She stood motionless and whimpered. Niles circled her, hissing and snarling.

I stood and rubbed at my wrists before holding out my hand. "I'll take that, thank you," I said, and used my magic to pull the pan from Trisha's grasp and into my own. I stared at it for a moment and then flicked out my other hand. Trisha screamed as she flew across the room and blasted into the wall before falling unconscious on the ground.

"You took your time," I said to Niles. He sat on his haunches and blinked at me. I pulled him into a deep hug, relishing the powerful presence of the panther. "Thank you," I said and glanced around the room. My eyes fell on the telephone and I pulled out of the hug.

"You'd better make yourself scarce," I said.

CHAPTER NINETEEN

I flicked the sign on the store door to open and pulled it wide. "Welcome to Crystal Magic," I said and ushered in our first guests.

"Can I offer you some refreshments?" Fleur practically bounced on her toes behind me.

I had to admit, inside I bounced, too. A line had formed outside for our grand reopening and a delightful parade of people entered the shop. We'd been lucky with the weather and everyone was in good spirits.

We dished out drinks and food and tried to cater to everyone's individual needs with our free samples. There was no use in handing out an oil that cured back pain if the person you gave it to didn't suffer from back pain in the first place.

"What's this?" The manager of the local café asked, lifting a beginner smoke-cleansing kit. Her name was Gemma, and she'd come along with her teenage daughter. I smiled and joined her by the kit. I didn't know what it was about the small bundle of dried lavender, the abalone shell, the strip of palo santo wood, and the feather that attracted people to it. Maybe it was the bright colour of the feather or the sparkly shell.

"Cleansing your home with lavender is a great way to cleanse it of stagnant and negative energy," I said, knowing this kit was extra special as I'd added a protection spell to keep evil spirits at bay. "You simply open a few doors and windows to help the negative energy leave, focus your intention, and then light the lavender, being sure to waft its smoke around all areas of your house using the feather. The kit includes full instructions on what to do."

"What are the shell and wooden stick for?" she asked, pulling the pack closer to her face and eyeballing the contents.

"The shell is a decorative fireproof vessel. You can light your lavender over it, and the wood you can light instead of the lavender. It carries the most delicious scent of lemon, pine, and mint. It brings healing and good fortune."

"Do they work?"

"I've always found them to be beneficial," I said. "A good cleansing does wonders for removing stress and creating a calming atmosphere. Why don't you take it home and see how you feel about it?"

Gemma beamed at me, but her eyes flicked around at the display Fleur and I had set out on the opposite side of the room. "Is it included in the samples you were giving out?" she asked.

"It is for you," I said, and winked. She'd been more than generous in giving us a local discount on all our food.

"Hey, Love," a man called from the sofa and waved at me before stuffing a piece of cake into his mouth.

Gemma leaned forward and whispered in my ear. "That's Andy. He runs the Goldcroft. He's a bit rough around the edges, but he'll be more than happy to send customers your way if he takes a shine to you."

Andy licked the remnants of chocolate from his fingers and nudged the man sitting beside him. "You got anything that can help with hallucinations? Peter here swears blind he saw a black panther on the common a few nights back after he left my place."

Fleur froze mid-serve behind him and shot me a worried glance. I walked over and put my hand on her shoulder before reaching for a sample. "Nothing for hallucinations," I said and tossed him the bottle. "But ginger here works wonders on hangovers."

Andy caught the bottle and laughed before tossing it to Peter and ruffling his hair. "Yep. That's what he needs. I keep telling him to stop mixing his beer and his whiskey, but he never listens." With that, he winked at me and grabbed another slice of cake.

Fleur relaxed with a sigh. She was the only person who knew that Niles had come to my rescue at Tanya's. I wanted her to know what she'd be letting herself in for if she bonded with Abby. She'd jumped at the idea, but I'd asked her to mull it over for a few days, and if she was certain, we'd do it on Sunday.

I turned to the sound of the newly repaired bell and saw Kate enter. Benjamin trailed behind her, looking clean, but unsure of himself. I walked over to greet them.

"Hi, I wasn't expecting you," I said. I hadn't seen Kate since she took my statement the night Trisha and Mrs Jenkins took me prisoner.

David had called in before he left for London. He had to get his car, but he also wanted to make sure I was okay and thank us for finding Julie's killer. He could leave for Canada knowing that the weight had finally been lifted from his shoulders.

"I ran into Benjamin and he wanted to come and see you," she said before turning to him and smiling. "I'm going to grab a piece of cake, and Fleur can help me find some of your fabulous ginseng tea," she said and left me standing alone with Benjamin.

"Thank you for finding my mum's killer," he said and rubbed the back of his neck nervously.

I patted him on the arm. "It was nothing."

He glanced back at the shelves put up to replace the ones he'd broken. "Sorry about…"

"It's fine. More importantly, how are you doing?"

"Good. Good. Mum didn't have a lot of money, but she left me the house in her will and that's mortgage-free. I've put it up for sale. Mrs Jenkins' house is on the market too, so I'm a little worried about how long it might take to sell. Susan has agreed to help with the funeral."

"That's something," I said.

"Yeah. I need to thank you there as well, actually. The quotes Trisha was giving me for the funeral costs were double the price they needed to be."

I offered Benjamin some tea and cake and suggested he look around. Any sample he wanted was his. He thanked me and said that he wasn't really into all this new age mumbo jumbo, but would take me up on the offer of a piece of cake.

He joined Fleur by the buffet and grabbed a piece of Victoria sponge. I eyed him curiously.

"I know that look," Kate said, coming over to stand beside me.

"What look?"

"The one that says you're about to meddle. We got the killer. You can relax. Mrs Jenkins is going to testify against Trisha. She might be trying for an insanity plea with all the nonsense about a panther, but it won't stick."

I nodded and bit my bottom lip. When the police had arrived to arrest Trisha and Mrs Jenkins, I explained how Mrs Jenkins had tried to save my life and managed to free me before being clocked over the head. The damage to the property had been the result of my ensuing struggle with Trisha. She'd insisted on the presence of a panther, but well... that was a result of delirium. She must have hit her head harder than I'd realised.

"I know that, but... there are still too many loose ends. Why did they take the cat?" I nodded towards Benjamin. "And why would Trisha try to overcharge him for the funeral when she knew Tanya didn't have any money to leave him?"

"Because you were right in your first guess when you said it was all about the money." Kate smiled and took a sip of tea.

"But it wasn't. It was about Julie's murder."

Kate shook her head. "It was about the money. Trisha's husband's business was going under. She'd asked Tanya for some money to help out, and she'd laughed in her face. They took her cat as a form of punishment. Mrs Jenkins said that Trisha wanted to remind her what it was like to lose something she loved. Trisha had been out shopping Wednesday morning and found the flyer offering the reward for Abby's safe return."

"She didn't know that Susan was paying the reward and not Tanya."

"That's right. She flew into a rage and that was that. Mrs Jenkins came home after visiting your store and found her standing over the body. Trisha convinced her that Tanya had fallen, but as they had taken the cat, she said no one would ever believe them. They decided to set the cat free and let you discover the body."

I sighed and shook my head. "You were right. I am no Miss Marple. I would have sworn it was related to Julie's killing."

"In a way, it was."

I nodded and sighed. Kate excused herself to mingle. I needed to get back to work, too. I'd left Fleur to hand out all the samples by herself for far too long. I'd have to give the girl a raise.

The night proved a roaring success. One by one, our guests left with bigger smiles on their faces than when they'd entered. On his way out, Peter thanked me for the ginger oil.

"You're welcome," I said.

Andy waved at his friend and shouted across the room. "Watch out for those panthers, mate."

Peter laughed and brushed his comment away, but my eyes darted to Kate, who tilted her head to the side in her curious dog-like pose. She raised an eyebrow. I smiled and shrugged.

~

CHAPTER ONE

A Word to the Witch (Book 2)

My hair puffed up around my head like a cotton ball and trailed down over my shoulder in great waves of dark brown. I huffed out a deep breath and stared at my reflection, lamenting my lack of products.

When Susan had suggested we accompany Gemma to her baking competition and make an event of the whole weekend by booking into the Celtic Manor Hotel, I'd jumped at the chance, especially when I heard we'd have time to enjoy the spa. What did it matter that we all lived less than five minutes away? A break was a break, and I hadn't taken one since moving to

Caerleon a few months ago. I deserved a little downtime.

"That's right." I gave a firm nod to my reflection. "You most certainly do." After solving a murder, relaunching the store, and training my apprentice, Fleur, I hadn't had time for a break, and I was determined to enjoy myself.

I sighed and slumped my shoulders, surveying the disaster that was my hair once again. I was due to meet Susan and Gemma in the bar in ten minutes. I had nowhere near enough time to pop home and grab some product. I still couldn't believe I'd failed to pack any. They should have been the first things in my bag. Although... I could always pop down to the hotel salon and see if they had anything that would make me look vaguely presentable. But given that it was almost 8 pm, I doubted they'd be open. No. There was nothing to do but tie it back. I delved into my bag, retrieved a hair tie and some pins, and decided to wrestle my unruly mane into a French plait. After a while, and a fair bit of cursing, I managed to create a plait/bun combo that didn't look too bad at all.

I glanced at the clock on the wall and noted I was running late. With one final check in the mirror, I surveyed my teeth for lipstick and, finding none, smoothed down the skirt of my tea-length pleated dress before grabbing my bag and heading out the door.

My pulse raced. I had to admit that I was more than a

little nervous as I paced along the corridor. The lush deep-blue carpet muffled my steps and made my heartbeat all the more noticeable. I smiled at a young couple as they passed and hoped it wasn't as obvious to them as it was to me.

Susan and Gemma were both new friends of mine, and I wanted more than anything for the weekend to go well. I couldn't remember a time in my life when I'd actually had 'girlfriends' or people I could go out and just have fun with. Susan, I'd met whilst investigating her friend Tanya's murder, and although I'd seen Gemma many times at her café, we'd become a lot closer after she and her daughter attended the reopening party for my store, Crystal Magic.

Susan met Gemma when I dragged her to the café for some much-needed sustenance after we'd enjoyed a movie and an abundance of vodka one night at her place. They'd hit it off immediately. It was Susan who persuaded Gemma to enter the baking competition. She'd become a firm favourite of Gemma's cooking after declaring her *mille-feuille* the best she had ever tasted. As soon as Gemma learned that was just posh for a cream slice, she was over the moon, although still a little reluctant to enter any competitions. Needless to say, we both soon learned how determined and persuasive Susan could be when she set her mind to something.

We'd arrived at the hotel and checked in at around two.

After ensuring everything was set up for Gemma tomorrow and discovering when and where she needed to report, we'd spent some time in the pool and then indulged in a massage as well as both a manicure and pedicure. We were all utterly relaxed afterwards and decided to grab a little shuteye before meeting up in the reception before heading to the court bar.

I pressed the button for the lift and waited for a few seconds, watching the light signalling where it was going. When I saw it highlight the floor below mine and then descend again, I tapped the button five more times and pulled my phone from my purse.

"Fleur," I said as soon as she answered. "I just wanted to make sure everything was alright."

"Relax and enjoy yourself," she said. "Everything's fine. Niles is making sure of that."

I smiled at the edge to her voice. At twenty, Fleur had come late to magic. Most start training from the moment they are born and have a familiar bound to them by their first birthday. Niles was my familiar. Abby, a little white floofball with a black puffy tail, had become Fleur's. But in much the same way Fleur was coming late to the game, so too was Abby, and to say that the cat had shown herself to be a little... shall we say, feisty with her newfound powers would be an understatement. I'd been reluctant to leave Fleur alone with her even for the weekend. When she reassured me that between her and Niles, they could stop Abby from turning into a leopard and terrorising the neighbours, I'd relented. I was only five minutes away if needed, after all, and have I mentioned how much in need of a break I was?

"Call if you need me," I said, and winced, dragging the phone away from my ear as Fleur bellowed at Abby to drop the sofa *this instant*. A loud thud followed. Remarkable strength was another of Abby's powers that she seemed to delight in. Last week, when Fleur made the mistake of closing the door when she took a bath, the rascal swiped it from its hinges.

"Eira, we'll be fine," Fleur said, returning her attention to our call.

"Just remember the exercises I taught you. If you keep her busy, I'm sure she'll stay entertained and out of trouble."

Fleur chuckled. "Niles has sat on her for the moment, and she seems pretty content to let him. I'll let them play for a while and try the exercises again later."

"Sounds like a plan." The lift pinged and the doors opened in front of me. "I've got to go. Don't forget to cal—"

"I know... I know. I'll call if I need you. Now go. Have fun."

I laughed, ended the conversation, and stepped inside the lift. It was good to have an apprentice, but even better to find a true friend in Fleur, even if she was half my age. It was shocking how quickly she'd become an essential part of my life. If things had been different with Abby, she'd be here now, enjoying the evening with us.

The ornate doors of the lift opened onto the opulent reception area, and the sound of chatter reached my ears. With the muffling carpet a thing of the past, I became conscious of the clip-clop of my heels on the tiled floor. I cleared my throat and tried not to fidget, convinced that everyone must be looking at me. I felt so out of place in the five-star resort. Susan informing me that she had once run into Johnny Depp in the restaurant way back in 2004 didn't help. Nor the fact that world leaders, including then US President Barack Obama, had visited in 2014 for a NATO Summit. Not to mention members of the royal family.

Mustering my courage, I glanced around but couldn't spot Susan or Gemma anywhere. I pulled my phone from my bag to check the time: 8:07 pm. I sighed and shook my head. I should have known that out of the three of us, I'd be the one closest to being on time. I walked to the circular lounge area in the middle of the reception and sat in a rich burgundy armchair that gave me a good view of both the lift and the doors to the outside. I smiled and sniffed at the vase of sunflowers in the middle of the accompanying coffee table before shifting the cushion behind my back to make myself more comfortable. A man in beige trousers and a baby blue shirt sat a few clusters over, engrossed with his phone. He must have felt my gaze as he lifted his head and nodded. His accompanying smile was warm and friendly, so I smiled back. Even though he returned his attention to his phone, his demeanour made me relax a little. Maybe I didn't look as out of place as I felt.

The entrance to the lobby banged open and an army of footsteps stomped the floor. I turned my attention to the commotion. A man had burst through the doors. Despite the ruckus that came with his appearance, he exuded a sense of calm and power. An entourage accompanied him, although security may be the more appropriate term. Four men flanked him, two on either side, all wearing the same black suits and skinny ties. I'd place them in their late twenties or early thirties, a good decade or two younger than the man they surrounded. They looked more than capable of military-style operations.

My head popped up. Even beneath the dark sunglasses and Panama hat, I recognised the man as Jeremy Dancer. I'd always admired the blend of muted gold and brown of his hair which shone like the Bruno Jasper stone. He wore it twisted in his signature bun.

This had to be the first time I'd been close to a real live celebrity, and although I wasn't normally one to swoon and fawn over such characters, my heart raced. Susan had mentioned the celebrity chef was one of the judges, but I imagined seeing him sat on a dais, lording over everyone and passing down judgement, not walking within ten feet of me. I found myself standing to get a better view, but blushed when the action caused him to notice me. He smiled and removed his sunglasses. My blush deepened.

He froze, his gaze never leaving my own. His mouth opened as if he was about to say something, and I wondered if I had a pen and paper in my purse should he ask if I wanted an autograph. Not that I did. It just felt rude of me not to be prepared should he offer.

A shrill call spared me embarrassment. All eyes rushed to the young woman in her mid-twenties who entered with an entourage of her own. She repeatedly shrieked Dancer's name and berated him for leaving her in the car, while flicking her long hair over her shoulder. An act all the more noticeable as her hair happened to be pink. I tried to place a stone or crystal that it most closely matched and couldn't. Rhodonite might come close, but I think bubble-gum-pink was a more apt description. The chef instantly deflated. All his confidence seemed to flee him in an instant. He turned to the woman in the sleek black dress and lifted his arms in mock surrender.

"I merely wanted to check in and gain our room key without the need for you to loiter in the foyer," he said in soothing tones.

The woman huffed and crossed her arms. She did not look

even slightly pleased. "You've dragged me to this God-forsaken place. The least you could do was help me out of the car with my things."

I raised an eyebrow and sat back down in my chair. Witnessing a domestic wasn't on my to-do list this weekend. Still, I couldn't help overhearing the exasperation in Jeremy Dancer's voice when he mentioned how he'd told her many times that she was more than welcome to stay home and that it was only by her insistence that she'd accompanied him.

She instantly turned on the waterworks, stamping her foot and blubbering like a two-year-old whose parents refused to let them eat a whole tub of ice-cream. She stepped closer to Jeremy. "Why don't you want me with you? Anyone would think you don't *love* me anymore," she said, her voice whiny but also carrying an unmistakable edge to her words.

I shrank further into my chair, embarrassed on behalf of all womanhood for her display, and pulled my phone from my bag again. 8:23. Come on, Gemma and Susan. Where are you, and why on Earth didn't we just meet up in the corridor outside our rooms? I glanced towards the lift and debated going to their rooms to fetch them. Only the fear of my footsteps echoing on the floor and drawing attention my way stilled my steps.

Out of the corner of my eye, I noticed Jeremy pull the woman in for a hug and whisper something in her ear. From the look that crossed her face, I could tell she felt as though she'd won something. He pulled away and landed a kiss on her lips before motioning to the seated area and suggesting she take a seat while he checked in.

My eyes darted around the lounge area. Accompanied as she was by her entourage, the only place she would have to sit was in the cluster of chairs between the man whose eyes were now glued to his phone as though his life depended on it and me.

I shouldn't have worried about her bodyguards. They stayed outside the lounge area and watched all points of entry to the room as though expecting an attack.

As she passed, she glared down her nose at me, and then lifted her chin and turned away as if disgusted by what she saw. I straightened my dress and clasped tightly onto my hands, telling myself it would be petty to use a little magic to make her fall on her smug face. In contrast, she turned her attention to the man in the blue shirt and flashed him a smile. Much to my amusement, he refused to even acknowledge her presence and instead pulled his phone closer to his face.

When she flashed me with a second look that indicated I was no better than something she might stand on in the street, I decided I'd had enough of waiting and no longer cared if the clip-clop of my heels drew attention. Plus, if I was honest with myself, the need to make some slight calamity befall the woman was becoming far too much of a temptation.

My hand flew to the Melody Stone around my neck. The sacred seven was made naturally from Amethyst, Cacoxenite, Rutile, Goethite, Clear Quartz, Smoky Quartz and Lepidocrocite. It enhanced my abilities to move objects. I'd crafted two pendants, one for me and one for Fleur, and insisted we wore them always. With it, we could move mountains. In theory. Not that I would need its power now. I just found it reassuring to know it was with me.

I could move the vase on the table without its help. I mean... a little nudge would see the flowers and water cascade over her...

No. I shook my head. Far better I left. I stood and walked back to the lift, keeping my head high and my gaze directly forward. Before I had the chance to reach the doors, they pinged open. Susan was mid-step out when I barrelled her back in.

"Eira," she barked when she almost stumbled into Gemma. "What *are* you doing?"

"Sorry," I said and slammed my finger into the close-door button. It was silly, I knew, but the last thing I wanted was to turn around now that I'd resolved to go to the lift. We could get off on another floor and walk around to the bar. "I'll explain later. There's a horrid woman in the lounge and I'd rather not have to look at her again."

Gemma puffed up and pushed past Susan. "What did she

do?" she demanded, and I had to grab hold of her arm to stop her charging through the doors.

"Nothing particularly," I said, inwardly smiling that Gemma seemed ready to fight for me.

She managed a quick glance out of the lift and then darted her head back inside before pressing the close-door button herself and selecting the next floor up. "Vanessa Brookes," was all she said as the doors finally closed, and the lift rumbled back to life.

"Who?" I asked.

"Really?" Susan said at the same time.

"Hmm, hmm, in the lounge. Real as life, wearing a black dress that couldn't be shorter if it were a belt."

"That's the horrid woman I told you about. Do you know her?"

"Do we know her?" Susan asked, her face incredulous. "How do you not?"

"Vanessa Brookes. The reality TV star. Her face is always on one magazine cover or another. Come on, you're bound to have seen her before," Gemma added.

I shrugged. "Not my sort of thing. But it doesn't matter anyway. Let's just get to the bar and enjoy our night. I'd much rather forget about ever laying eyes on Vanessa Brookes or whatever her name is and have fun just as we'd planned. She can go her merry way with Jeremy Dancer, and we can go ours."

"Jeremy Dancer," Gemma said and looked for all the world as though she might press the button to send the lift back down to the reception. "We missed everything."

"She was with Jeremy?" Susan asked. Her face looked a little sad, and a pang of guilt overtook me. I'd selfishly forced them both back into the lift because I'd been uncomfortable. So, what if I hadn't wanted to gawp at celebrities? Well… any more than I already had. That didn't mean I had the right to deprive my friends of the privilege.

"I'm sure we'll get the chance to see them together tomorrow at the competition," I said. "Jeremy is a judge, after all."

Susan flashed me a smile that didn't quite reach her eyes. "Of course. Let's get that drink," she said, and looped her arms between mine and Gemma's just as the lift doors opened.

~

VICTORIADELUIS

Printed in Great Britain
by Amazon